Worth the Wait

by

Annie Seaton

Dedication

This book is dedicated to those friends and colleagues who supported me in my Jaclyn days. You know who you are. I was given lemons and I made lemonade... and a whole new career as an author!

Chapter 1

"Who the frig are you, love? All dolled up with nowhere to go in this hick town!"

The husky chuckle and the smell of cigarette smoke stopped Jaclyn Douglas about a metre short of the front gate of Bindarra Creek Central School. A teenager—his face half-covered by a black hoodie—was sitting in the garden beneath a demountable building, a few metres to the left of the entry to the administration office where she was headed. Jaclyn walked to the gate and looked over at the young man as he put the cigarette to his mouth and drew in deeply. A pair of defiant eyes held hers as he looked over at her.

"I would say the question is more 'where should you be?'" Jaclyn looked down at the elegant gold watch on her wrist with a frown. "I believe Bindarra Creek Central has a six-period day, and lunch has just passed, so my guess is it's period five and you should be in class."

"Don't like friggin' maths and besides Old Curly should have carked it by now. He's so fuc—I mean bloody boring." The boy's eyes narrowed as he looked at her above the low metal gate. He ran his gaze up from Jaclyn's shoes to the white blouse tucked neatly into her pencil-slim navy skirt. "How do *you* know about how many periods we have anyway?"

"I suggest that if you wish to redeem yourself in the eyes of your principal, that you put that cigarette out, put the butt in the bin, and get yourself off to Mr Curlew's class now."

"Nuh. We don't have a real principal anymore. Kev won the lottery and was out of this dump like a shot." A plume of smoke surrounded the boy and Jaclyn stifled a grin; he thought he was pretty tough. "Half his luck," he continued. "It was his ticket out of this hick town. 'Derro' Dave's been filling in for a couple of weeks and he's a piece of —"

"Mr Parch!" a voice roared through the window before Jaclyn could hear what Dave was a piece of, but she had a fair idea from the boy's expression.

Both the young smoker and Jaclyn jumped as a man's head appeared through the window of the demountable. "Get yourself in here this instant!"

"Shit. Sprung." The boy ground the cigarette

into the garden and jumped to his feet. His hoodie fell back revealing a scrawny face and narrow nose, but it was the yellow and purple bruise on the side of his face that caught Jaclyn's attention. He took off at a run and before she could call out to him, he'd disappeared around the back of the temporary building.

The window slammed shut, and the glass rattled.

Jaclyn pushed open the rusted gate that led from the car park to the school and bit back her frustration as it creaked and jammed half-open. She shoved it and loose rust came off onto her hand.

How much would it cost to put a decent gate at the entry of the school? She knew it wasn't the school's fault; it was simply a shortage of adequate maintenance funding. The small schools out west— indeed most schools outside the metropolitan area— had to fight for a share of the dwindling bucket of money for public education. She thought of her last school—Sanctuary Gardens High School— not only was it in a rich Sydney suburb, but it had the advantage of being situated in a marginal seat for the sitting member and there had never been a shortage of money for building work or teaching staff. It was a sign of the times that it had taken a fire at a country school to get attention from those who held the education purse strings.

Jaclyn paused and took a deep breath. There would be time to address those issues; this was *not* the time to get upset. She'd spent way too much of her work—and personal—time stressing over the past few months and in her late thirties, Jaclyn knew she had to learn to put things into perspective.

But it was so hard.

She started walking again, this time with purpose in her step. While she was at Bindarra Creek Central School she *would* make a difference—even if it took the full three years of her tenure. It didn't matter if it was a small school in a country town. Okay, it might be very different to where she'd come from, but that choice had been taken from her.

She'd been directed to report to the regional office on the North Shore for admin duties, and then at the last minute Kevin Strickland, the principal at Bindarra Creek, had won the lottery, and she'd been offered this school. There were issues that needed immediate attention after the fire a couple of months ago, so they had wanted a permanent principal appointed immediately, rather than waiting until the new school year.

Jaclyn glanced over at the police-taped building at the side of the school. It was lucky for the town and the students that the fire had been controlled before it reached the primary school building. As well as the demountable building at the front of the school, two more temporary buildings had been placed on the school sports oval until the buildings were replaced.

As the rusted gate creaked closed behind her, the heels of her corporate navy-blue shoes clicked on the overgrown path, and Jaclyn's spirits sank as she surveyed the Bindarra Creek schoolgrounds. Someone had tried to brighten the gardens at the edge of the path with pots of flowers, but the winter just past had left them withered and brown.

Her previous school, Sanctuary Gardens High School, had boasted a full-time gardener as well as a general assistant to do the school repairs, not to mention the steady stream of contractors who were always there to make the school an attractive and quality learning environment.

Nothing to do with education, but all with the goal of getting the sitting member re-elected. She looked around; maybe past circumstances had fed her cynicism, but it was obvious that this town was part of a safe government seat.

Sanctuary Gardens High School had been surrounded by a high security fence; nothing like the broken wire fence with rotten posts that ran from the rusted gate to the corner of the building in front of her. Peeling paint and brown grass sent her mood plummeting even lower. She didn't want to be here, and to face such a depressing physical environment was going to make the three years here even harder.

If it hadn't been for—

Jaclyn pushed open the door into the foyer of the school. Stepping across to the enquiry counter, she waited to be attended to. An overweight woman with frizzy ginger hair was on the phone with her back to the window, and Jaclyn looked around the office as she waited for the office assistant to finish the call. The foyer was carpeted in a dull brown carpet and the walls were painted in a depressing yellow. A sad pot plant drooped in one corner, and Jaclyn could almost hear it begging for water as a stale smell pervaded the space.

"Jeez Louise. Not Izzy Black too!"

Jaclyn's eyebrows rose as the telephone conversation continued.

"That bloody Brett has been giving Jules the run around for too long. How long do you reckon it'll be before she wakes up to the fact that he's doing the dirty on her?" The office girl twirled the phone cord around her hand. "No way. It's not up to me to tell her that her husband's playing around. You've been friends with her longer than me. *You* tell her."

A young woman with brown curly hair walked into the office from a side entrance and glanced across at Jaclyn. She held the hand of a small girl and the child smiled at Jaclyn as they passed the counter where she stood.

"That's a pretty lady, Miss Mandy," she said loudly to the woman who held her hand.

Jaclyn smiled at the little girl and the child looked down shyly. They went across to a cupboard and the woman opened the door and pointed to the middle shelf. "Can you see the red paper, Selina?"

The child nodded. "I can."

"Can you count out three pieces for me?"

"She needs to know before she springs them." The office assistant continued her phone conversation and the other woman looked embarrassed as she glanced over at Jaclyn again.

"That's one . . . two . . . three!" The little girl slowly counted out three pieces of paper and handed them over.

"And then he was chatting up Raelene at the pub last night. Rog told me." The voice was getting louder, and Jaclyn pursed her lips. As she drew herself to her full height and took a deep breath, the foyer door opened and closed behind her, and the young teacher glanced her way. As she walked across the office with the little girl, the woman touched the shoulder of the office assistant.

"Counter, Kel," she said. "Two waiting." Her voice was quiet, but Jaclyn heard the words and nodded her thanks.

"We went there for a feed and—" The woman swivelled in her chair and saw Jaclyn at the counter. "Shit, love. Gotta go. I'll ring you back in ten." She pushed the chair back and as she walked slowly across to the window. "Yeah?" She opened her mouth and removed a piece of chewing gum and put it in the bin beneath the counter.

"I'm Jaclyn Douglas. Your new principal."

If it hadn't been unprofessional, Jaclyn would have laughed at the stunned expression on the woman's face when she introduced herself.

Chapter 2

Ryan Rossiter opened the door, entered the foyer and glanced at the back of the tall blonde woman waiting at the counter.

Why did every blonde woman have to remind him of Jaclyn Douglas?

It was time he got over it. An uneasy feeling tugged at him; his grandmother would have called the prickling on his neck a premonition. Ryan shrugged it off; it was from the heat of being cooped up in the ute for the long trip from Sydney.

It couldn't be.

Last time he'd be doing that trip for a long while. A contented smile crossed his face as the door closed silently behind him. He'd been commuting from the Sydney office to Bindarra Creek for three months, and staying out at his farm on the weekends, but last weekend he'd moved here to stay.

He cringed as he listened to Kellie's phone conversation. Ryan had spent a bit of time at the school because of the number of building works needed, and he'd written up a preliminary inspection report on the damaged high school block.

Lea wasn't in the office, and Kellie hadn't noticed the woman waiting at the counter yet. Mandy, the teacher's aide who he'd met at the pub last Saturday, looked over and caught his eye, and he nodded towards the woman waiting. Mandy nodded back and touched Kellie's shoulder on her way to the door.

Kellie pushed herself to her feet and came across to the counter. Ryan's stomach sank when the woman in front of him spoke, and he widened his eyes, unable to believe what he was hearing

Who he was hearing.

He ignored the increase in his heat rate.

"Good afternoon. I'm Jaclyn Douglas. I believe you are expecting me?"

Bloody Nora! What the hell is she doing here?

As soon as he'd heard her voice, Ryan knew it was Jaclyn; he didn't even have to wait to hear her name. Her voice was instantly recognisable along with the plummy tone. Kellie's eyes widened and he felt sorry for her.

"Oh, um . . . g'day, love. . . I mean welcome, Mrs . . . Miss . . . um, anyway hello. Ah, Lea's off sick today. Well, she's not sick, David is. Not David the deputy, David, her husband. We . . . um . . . thought you weren't arriving until next week.

14

We've ordered a cake for morning tea on Monday. We can't get it now because Cleo Kendall is making it and she and Jonathon live way out of town." She glanced across at Ryan. "You know Cleo, don't you, Ryan? She's been doing cooking for functions in town since she—"

The familiar voice was crisp as Jaclyn put her hand up, obviously to stop the flow of words that were streaming from Kellie's—without chewing gum—mouth.

"I arrived early."

That'd be right, thought Ryan. No explanation, no warmth, no sympathy for poor Kellie who'd been caught out in a personal conversation.

Exactly what he'd expect from Jaclyn Douglas these days. Once he'd thought she was a good person—and maybe a little bit more than that— but she had changed. He wondered why she was out here at Bindarra Creek anyway. He'd hadn't heard a whisper about her coming, even at the local regional office. But as it was only two weeks since Kevin Strickland had left, he wasn't surprised that word hadn't got around.

What the heck was she doing here? And Kellie had said they were expecting her Monday? Maybe she was here to run one of those inspection programs.

There was no way a city girl like Jaclyn would

stay out here for long. Bindarra Creek was far removed from the trendy restaurants and wine bars of North Sydney. And a very different school to the large school she'd been appointed to in Sydney when they'd been seeing each other.

Why the hell would she be out west when she had a school to run in the city?

He'd noticed the black Audi TT parked near the gate when he'd got out of his work ute, but taken no notice. As he'd lifted his keys to lock the door of his work ute, a movement caught his eye. A school student—male and skinny—had been sneaking around the side of the building and as Ryan watched, the boy ran across the concrete quadrangle making a beeline for the low fence. In one lithe movement he'd jumped over the sagging wire onto the footpath and headed for the Audi. Ryan was out of the boy's line of vision, although with the hoodie pulled across his face, he would have been flat out seeing anything to either side. Ryan stood by his vehicle and waited to see what the boy was up to. His body language hinted he was up to no good.

"Bloody hell." The words had been followed by a low appreciative whistle as the boy furtively approached the sports car.

Ryan had stepped out and walked around the front of the ute. "Nice car. Hey?"

The boy jumped and looked poised for flight

but had stayed there when he decided Ryan obviously wasn't a threat.

"Yeah, it's okay, but no good for the crap roads out here. Who'd bring a city car like this to this shithole? If I had a car like that, I'd only drive it on the freeway."

Ryan had shrugged as he clicked the electronic lock of this vehicle. If he'd recognised the Audi as Jaclyn's, he would have been more prepared to see her. The kid had been right. Jaclyn Douglas was a city slicker who wouldn't be seen dead in the country.

"True," he'd said. "It'll need a wash sooner than later."

"No point. Waste of effort out here." The boy shrugged and took off across the sports field without a backward glance.

"And a waste of water," Ryan thought as he'd put his keys in his pocket and headed up the path to the school.

He stood straight as he now waited unashamedly to hear what else Jaclyn had to say, but she turned to see who Kellie had been talking to. To his satisfaction, her eyes widened for a fleeting instant before she reverted to her ice queen composure.

"Ryan . . . ah, Mr Rossiter." A terse nod with a wrinkling of her brow. "What are you doing here?"

Before Ryan could answer, a man with long hair pulled messily back into a ponytail poked his head around the corner of the internal door into the office. "Kel, be a love and go up the street and get me a coffee and a cream bun."

"Ah, Dave, not at the moment," Kellie said. "I'm a bit busy. You'd better come and meet the new—"

"Bloody hell, I'll go and get it myself." He disappeared, and the sound of a door slamming rattled the windows of the small office.

Ryan felt sorry for Kellie and he tried to take Jaclyn's attention away from her. "Ms Douglas, I'm here to inspect the high school building block."

"That won't be necessary now that I've arrived," she said.

Any sympathy Ryan felt, disappeared as his temper began a slow burn. He stepped closer and folded his arms, and Kellie's head swivelled from Jaclyn to him, and then back to her again.

"Well, I would have to disagree with that statement." He could talk posh too when necessary. "I must inform you that it *is* essential and is the main part of my brief. I've been sent here by the regional Properties Department to do a site survey and advise on the need for demolition or restoration, and I will be doing exactly that." His voice was firm as he held the cold gaze, and he bit back the stronger words that he wanted to add.

"And I've been sent here to ensure that we *demolish* and rebuild." Her arms folded, and her chin went up. She was tall, and her eyes were almost level with his. For a brief second, Ryan thought he'd seen a flash of uncertainty in her eyes—the eyes that had once attracted him—and then as they turned back to cold and steely green, he knew he'd imagined it. He'd seen Jaclyn in operation before, and this confrontation wasn't going to be pretty. The difference was this time he knew not to trust her.

"Well, then," he said. "I guess we'd better make some phone calls because I'm not leaving."

"Neither am I." Her voice was as cold as her eyes. After a pointed glance at Kellie, she lifted her head and stared at him. "Perhaps you would be kind enough to show me to *my* office so I can meet with Mr Rossiter?"

"Your office?" he asked.

What a hide. She expected her own office to deal with the building issue. Ryan could tell Ms Douglas what was happening, and she could hightail it back to Sydney right now.

"Yes. The principal's office. I've been appointed to Bindarra Creek Central."

*****

Even though a glimmer of sympathy for both

the office girl and Ryan rippled through Jaclyn, she kept her expression bland as she followed Kellie along the corridor to the principal's office. The same dull brown carpet lined the narrow floor, and paint peeled off the walls, and even worse, the odour of damp carpet gone mouldy pervaded the space.

"Sorry about the smell," Kellie said. "Lea usually has a diffuser going but we ran out of the lemon myrtle oil yesterday. The carpet got wet when we had the flood back in winter, and it's been getting more of a stink up as the weather gets hotter."

Jaclyn's temper began to build; whoever had been in charge of this school up to this point had not fought for a fair go. Even though money was always short in schools, an effective leader *could* make a difference and chase up funding through grants.

And fast.

The ruined carpet should have been replaced on an insurance claim immediately.

"That smell is a WHS issue," she said primly.

They reached the door of an office at the far end of the gloomy corridor. On the door, a black sign in a narrow slot identified the room as the *Principal's Office*. Kellie stopped suddenly before they reached it. She held her hands out in front of her as she looked at Jaclyn, as though to stop her, and then dropped her gaze to the floor.

"Dave hasn't moved out of the office yet. Maybe it would be better if you go into the kitchen and have your meeting?" Her words were hopeful.

"Dave? The I-want-you-to-get-me a-coffee-and cream-bun man?" Jaclyn resisted turning around as a muffled snort came from Ryan Rossiter who had followed them up the corridor. "Dave is the acting principal?"

"Um, yes. We were going to sort the office out today and tomorrow, but Lea's not here. And um, I've been busy manning the counter and the phones." Kellie flushed brick red and nodded vigorously, and her frizzy hair went out in a cloud. "She did ring up and tell us to make sure we got it sorted this afternoon. And I was going to, as soon as I got off the phone. Dave's going back to the maths staff room. We just didn't think you'd be here today." Her eyes brightened as she stared at Jaclyn, and then Ryan. "I know! Why don't you go up the street and have a coffee together? It'd be much nicer than in the office. Ryan, you take Mrs Douglas to the Levonis's café and have your meeting there. I'll help Dave sort the office while you're gone." By this stage the office assistant had her back against the office door and was barricading the entry with her ample bulk.

"It's *Ms* Douglas not Mrs," Jaclyn said and

shook her head. "And I will meet with Mr Rossiter in *my* office now."

Kellie's voice was almost a squeak, her eyes wide. "They have really good cakes there, don't they, Ryan? Baklava, if you're in luck." She looked at her watch and frowned. "You might be a bit late, but they always have plenty of other great stuff. I keep telling Thalia they don't make enough to last the day."

Jaclyn fought the lifted eyebrow that threatened.

Ryan? It sounded as though Mr Ryan Rossiter was already known at the school. She'd assumed it was his first visit too. Confusion filled her; why had they sent an assessor from the Sydney office when there was a perfectly good regional office in Tamworth? And how did they know him by name already? And more confusing, why was he so fired up about restoration, when her email had definitely said demolition was the preferred option?

"This will be quite suitable," she said. "Open the door—please." Jaclyn frowned as Kellie rolled her eyes and pushed the door open.

Forget about building demolition or restoration, the first thing she was going to have to do was work on this space that was supposed to be the principal's office. Two bean bags sat in the middle of the threadbare brown carpet, and a row of used takeaway coffee containers lined the edge of the large desk. Despite the state of the room, she gestured to the chair and moved around to sit at the business side of the desk. Kellie—another issue she would have to deal with sooner than later—backed out of the room and closed the door with a dissatisfied slam.

Always expert at hiding her feelings, Jaclyn kept her face expressionless as Ryan Rossiter took the chair she indicated. Jaclyn had over thirty years of practice at building up her shell and she was a master at self-protection. A recalcitrant office assistant, and an office that looked more like a games room, were not going to faze her, nor was the extremely good-looking man who was now observing her across the width of the desk.

That attraction had died a sudden death three months ago when her life had taken a downward turn.

Jaclyn reached over and clicked the mouse to close the game of solitaire that was open on the desktop, and despite her growing temper she sat straight and folded her hands neatly together on the desk in front of her as she looked calmly at Ryan Rossiter.

His mouth twitched, and she knew he was amused by the situation, so she got straight to business. "It appears that you've had a wasted trip to Bindarra Creek, Mr Rossiter—"

"Ryan, please Jac. Don't be silly," he said. "There's no need to be formal."

"It appears you've had a long and wasted trip, Mr Rossiter." The twitch disappeared from his mouth as it settled into a straight line when she ignored his request and the shortening of her name.

He settled back into his chair. "It certainly wasn't wasted, *Ms* Douglas."

"Oh, and why would you say that?" she asked. "Bindarra Creek is a long way from the city."

His smile was smug. "That it may be, but it's where I live now."

Jaclyn tipped her head to the side and blinked to cover her reaction. Her voice was even as she replied. "You live here?"

He nodded. "I've been transferred to the North West Region. I'm here to stay. This is my *home* now."

"I am here to stay too." Heat warmed her cheeks and she swallowed. "I've been appointed to the position at Bindarra Creek for a three-year tenure, so I won't be going anywhere until the buildings are replaced. *And* until I bring this school up to standard. It certainly appears to need it, and not just in rebuilding." Her voice had an edge to it, and the unusual lack of control over her emotional reaction fired Jaclyn's temper further. Heat spread through her body, and she moved her hands down, gripping them tightly on her lap beneath the desk. "And the buildings will be demolished and rebuilt."

Ryan leaned forward, and she was pleased to see a flush high on his cheeks. "And tell me, *Ms* Douglas, have you already had time to inspect them? I was under the impression that you had just arrived at the school in your fancy car."

For the first time in a long time, words deserted Jaclyn, so she focused her gaze on him and kept her expression cold. The silence grew and he folded his arms as he kept his eyes locked with hers.

It was broken when the door flew open and they both jumped as David Kepple, the former acting principal, stood in the doorway clutching a takeaway coffee container in one hand and a brown paper bag in the other.

"Um, can I have my office back now?"

Chapter 3

Ryan turned his ute onto the Tamworth road and headed out of town. He glanced at the fuel gauge as he passed Fred's Garage, and decided he had enough diesel to get out to the farm and then back to town tomorrow. Living twenty kilometres out suited him; he loved living on the land.

His land.

Since the rain that had soaked the district in the winter, and the ensuing flash flood that had almost resulted in tragedy, his property was lush and green despite the widespread drought. He was being careful, the rain had stayed away, and he wasn't prepared to stock his property yet. He had time to wait now that he'd moved here.

When the ridiculous situation at the school with the ice queen principal had reached a stalemate and she'd reluctantly vacated the office so it could be prepared for her takeover, Ryan had followed Jaclyn back to the foyer. He'd lifted his gaze as he found his eyes wandering to the smooth curves revealed by her snug-fitting skirt. Not matter how hard Jaclyn's character was, she was a fine-looking woman.

That surprising twinge of sympathy had tugged

at him at the reception she'd received at the school, but he'd pushed it away. Jaclyn was as hard as nails; he'd seen her in action in the city when she'd ripped a plumbing contractor to pieces in a meeting. Okay, the guy might have deserved it, but there'd been no need to be so harsh in a public forum.

If there was one thing Ryan hated, it was aggression. He and his brother, Joe, had had enough of that growing up on the farm at Werris Creek. Their stepfather had been a cruel man, and Ryan had hated seeing Jaclyn having scant regard for the feelings of others.

He tried to forget that the guy she'd ripped into had been dishonest and had caused a heap of grief for her school. She could have dealt with him in a softer way.

That night at dinner, he'd made the mistake of telling her she'd been too harsh.

That had gone down *really* well.

Not.

So when Jaclyn Douglas had suddenly wanted to climb the greasy pole of success, Ryan knew she was not the woman for him.

Now he had to cope with her here in Bindarra Creek, and he wasn't happy about it. Ryan tapped his fingers on the steering wheel as the wheels shuddered on the corrugations in the dirt road. She must have really upset someone higher up the pole to be given a posting out to a small central school in the west. Last he'd heard she was supposed to be moving from Sanctuary Gardens—where she'd only been for a couple of months—into the state office in the city. She'd been the golden-haired girl and destined for fast promotion if the department gossip mill could be believed.

Ryan shrugged as he approached the gate of his new property; it was after three-thirty and he'd clocked off for the day. He had enough of his own problems to sort out here than have time to worry about a woman who'd dismissed him with a curt command in the school foyer.

"Come back and see me tomorrow," she'd said in that imperious voice.

Well, Ms Douglas, I'll be back, don't you worry about that. All he had done was given her a curt nod before he made an appointment for the following afternoon, even though Kellie had told him just to turn up.

"Kevin never had appointments," she said.

"Make me one please, Kellie. I think you might find things will become a little bit more citified from now on."

Ryan was determined to meet with Jaclyn and establish a professional relationship that would allow them to discuss the problem at hand: the decision to either demolish or restore the high school buildings that had been damaged by fire earlier in the year. A new general-purpose building had already been built for years seven to ten, but the reason he was here was to assess the damaged buildings. If Jaclyn thought she could waltz in here and make a decision to demolish with no inspection or consultation, she had a few shocks ahead.

It didn't matter that Ryan was hoping that the buildings could be restored; a feasibility study had to be undertaken, and the bottom line was that the cost of rebuilding or restoration would be the factor that guided the final decision. The original high school buildings—currently roped off with some of the blue and white blue police tape still clinging to the rope—were a part of the history of the town, and he knew that most of the townspeople were hoping for restoration. He had sat in on a P &C meeting last month and there had been very strong opinions put forward. He was coming back to the P&C meeting next week to reassure the community.

Ryan had had many non-work conversations with the locals since he'd bought his property six months ago. Bindarra Creek had done it tough in recent years, and he knew that demolishing the old buildings would leave yet another scar on the town. If there was any way he could ensure that they followed the path of restoration, he would do that. That's what the townsfolk wanted, and that's what was needed. He just hoped he could deliver that with his assessment of the damage to the buildings.

Even if it meant working with the difficult *Ms Douglas*. Even if it meant trying to convince her that demolition was the last option he would consider.

Ryan was usually a good judge of character, but boy, had he made the wrong call with Jaclyn. Again, he wondered what she was doing out here. Something didn't feel right, and she'd certainly looked stressed. He mulled over the problem as he turned off the main road onto Rossiter's Lane.

He'd found the property online, and when he'd come out to see it the first time and seen that it had his family name, he knew it was meant to be. His decision had been swift, and settlement had gone through without a hitch. He'd now been the proud owner—with the bank—of Rossiter's Run for three months. He didn't know much about his birth father's family, but when he had time he vowed to find out if there was a connection to his property.

Ryan slowed the car and frowned as he approached his northern boundary fence. He glanced at the front paddock and the few fat steers he had there. It was the time of day for him to forget about work, forget about the new principal, and the school building problems. He had enough problems of his own to sort out here on Rossiter's Run.

He turned into the drive and headed towards the house where he was bunking down, surprised to see another ute parked near the old rundown building.

As he parked beside the ute his smile widened. It was Joe's ute.

He parked the Toyota, climbed out and slammed the door just as his little brother walked out of the farmhouse.

Ryan grinned. *If you could call it that, but one day it would be.*

"Hey, Joey! What are you doing here?"

His younger brother grabbed him in a brief man hug. It had been a few months since they'd last caught up. "I came to check out this new farm you reckon was worth spending your hard-earned cash on, bro." Joe grinned as he looked around. "You've done well, what a great piece of land."

"I'm pretty stoked with it," Ryan said. "A fair way out of town, but I don't see a problem with that."

"I'm with you.," Joe said. "I've just spent a couple of weeks in Sydney. Never again. I'm a country boy. But twenty ks is nothing."

"Yeah, me too. But as well as running the place, I've still got a day job to work at for a few more years yet." Ryan reached into the back of the ute and pulled out his briefcase. He looked at it ruefully. "I'd love to be in the position of just working the farm.”

“Small steps, mate. Remember, Rome wasn’t built in a day. Either that or win Lotto.”

“I wish.”

“What’s your plan? Are you going to get some sheep too?”

“Why? You want to come shearing here?” Ryan grinned at Joe. He was proud of his little brother; he was one of the top shearers in the north west.

“Be okay. So you will grow wool?”

“Eventually, once the drought is over.”

“Yeah, I couldn’t believe it when I drove from Armidale to Tamworth this week,” Joe said as they walked towards the homestead. “The sheep are on bare dirt, and there’s no feed to be seen.”

“I know. Things are grim, and the dams are dry too.” Ryan nodded. “Anyway, let’s hope it rains soon. I’ve got a few months of work ahead. I have to get those front paddocks fenced before I can get some more stock on the place.” As he turned towards his home, the afternoon sun softened the faded grey of the bare weatherboards on the house and glinted on those front windows that still had glass in them. With summer approaching fast, Ryan had bunked down in the two rooms at the back of the house; all he needed was his swag and the portable barbeque he’d set up outside. It was warm enough to wash in the creek that ran along the back fence, and the old dunny in the back yard was still usable. After spending three years in the city, roughing it here on the land—his land—was living the dream. And there was plenty of room for Joe to stay.

"You happy to bunk in your swag, Joe?" Ryan frowned as Jaclyn's face came into his thoughts. He wondered where she was living. In the city, she'd had a great apartment overlooking the harbour. He pushed away the image that had stayed with him all the way from town. The image of her pretty face, and long blonde hair, and those soft pink lips that he'd once kissed. In the days before Jaclyn had turned from him. Today those pretty lips had been set in a straight line.

She'd pulled the wool over his eyes for too long; he'd been a gullible fool. There must have been something she'd wanted from him when they'd been seeing each other, but for the life of him Ryan still didn't know what it could have been. He frowned; they had had five months together and it had been fun while it lasted. They'd enjoyed doing the same things, had the same taste in offbeat movies, and jazz and blues music, and had spent a few weekends together at concerts in the Hunter Valley vineyards.

If he was honest, it had been a great few months.

Ryan jumped as his brother's voice interrupted his musing.

"I am."

"You are what?"

"Happy to bunk in my swag. Earth to Ryan?" Joe stared at him. "Anyone home?"

"Sorry, I was thinking about work today."

"Well, I think a beer's in order. What say you?"

Ryan brought his mind back to the present and nodded with a grin. "I say what are we waiting for? Sounds good to me."

***

From the moment she'd encountered the recalcitrant student when she'd arrived at Bindarra Central School, Jaclyn's mood had worsened with each subsequent encounter. It was easier to leave them to the office clean up than to give in to the words that were trying to escape her set lips. Her Audi beeped as she unlocked it with the remote and she got into the car with a weary heart.

What had she done? Why was she out here? A long way from everything that was familiar to her, trying to put on a brave face and be the firm decisive person that most of her education colleagues thought she was.

But she wasn't, and for the first time since she'd left Sydney the day before yesterday, Jaclyn wondered if she really was strong enough to do this.

She was tired; not just physically after the long drive, but a bone-wearying despair had settled into her soul. Maybe she should have resigned and not taken the appointment out to Hicksville. She rested her head back on the soft leather head rest and allowed herself a moment to close her eyes. The situation she had faced in her last school had culminated in an ultimatum. No matter how unfair it had been, it had been out of her control.

Her choices: move into state office and be demoted to the position of deputy principal at a large school in the city when a position became available or continue her principal's career in a smaller central school in the boondocks.

This position had come out of the blue when the previous principal had left here with little notice. So, less than a week after she left her office at Sanctuary Gardens High School, here she was in Bindarra Creek, a long way further west than she'd ever been before. She had arrived a couple of days before she had expected to—the trip from Sydney had been shorter than she'd read on the map—and, as she realised now when she started the ignition of her totally out of place sports car, she had nowhere to stay. A hurriedly packed suitcase sat on the back seat beside her coffee maker, her briefcase and laptop bag next to it; the sum total of her planning— she hadn't been thinking straight.

Finding somewhere to stay until she settled into the school—and the town—was her first task. While she focused on what had to be done, she could keep it together. Seeing Ryan Rossiter had been the hardest part of the day, not to mention the fact that she would be working closely with him over the next few months.

Tears threatened as the ache in her throat intensified.

Forget Ryan; he had been another one in the long line of people who'd let her down. Judged her and found her wanting. She'd thought Ryan was different, and that she could trust him, but even before things went pear-shaped, he'd judged her. They'd had fun together when they'd been seeing each other; he'd made her laugh, and he'd put no pressure on her. Sharing a room and sleeping together had come after a couple of months of dinner dates and on their second weekend away to the vineyards. Jaclyn had been touched by his shyness at dinner a week before the trip away.

"Um, Jac? I've been thinking." Ryan had tapped his fork nervously on the table as he'd stared at her. He dropped his head and that recalcitrant lock of hair had fallen forward and she'd been tempted to reach over and push it back.

Jaclyn had tilted her head to the side and smiled. She'd gotten very used to looking at Ryan over the past few weeks. His face was tanned, and he had a cute dimple in the centre of his chin. Staring into gorgeous blue eyes surrounded by lush lashes as dark as his hair made her tremble inside.

"About?" she'd asked.

"The Hunter Valley trip. What do you say about sharing a room?"

As she'd reached forward and slowly pushed back that lock of hair, his eyes had lit up in a smile.

"I'd say I didn't think you were ever going to ask," she'd whispered.

The next three months they had spent most of their free time together, and Jaclyn had been happier than she had been for a long time. Until Ryan had fronted her that last night, she hadn't been able to believe what she'd heard.

A good lesson in life. You couldn't trust anyone.

Ryan had gone, and then her career hit the skids, and she had no one to turn to.

Her fast exit from Sydney had been her way of coping with the situation and she had little memory of the two-day trip west. Now she forced herself to open her eyes—she couldn't sit in the school car park for the rest of the afternoon—she had to find herself somewhere to stay for a few days, until she could organise a more permanent lodging.

The car started with a soft purr and a glimmer of peaceful familiarity descended.

One day at a time; that's how I'll survive out here.

If she kept herself busy—and by a quick look at the school—and the staff, and the students, as well as the brief interaction in the office—she knew there *was* plenty to do and the time would pass quickly.

Jaclyn glanced in the rear vision mirror and the Audi pulled out onto the road. As she headed along the street past the sports oval—she ignored the students out there without a teacher in sight—before she realised she had no idea where she was going. The roads were empty and there was no one on the footpath or in their gardens to ask for directions. It was so different to the bustle of the city. It wasn't that big a place, she'd find what she was looking for.

Jaclyn swallowed; she knew she could cope with the change. She'd have to; she had no choice.

As an intersection approached, she leaned forward; there was a park on her left—Lette Park the sign read—and there seemed to be a business area to the right. She indicated and turned and immediately noticed a sign for a carpark on the right. Indicating again she pulled into the almost empty lot. Yes, there was a newsagency and a bakery across the road and a supermarket next to the small car park.

Surely someone could direct her to the information centre?

Jaclyn climbed from the Audi and glanced at the tinted window; it was impossible to see her laptop on the back seat. Clicking the remote, the car locked with a quiet snick and she glanced left and right, waiting for a dusty ute to go past before she crossed the wide street. There was a wooden seat outside the newsagency, and two elderly gentlemen watched as she crossed the road.

Pausing in front of them, she waited until they stopped their conversation and looked at her curiously.

"Ah, excuse me. Could you direct me to the information centre, please?" Jaclyn smiled brightly, but the chuckle that came from both men was not what she expected.

"What do ya reckon, Charlie?" the one on the left said with a slow shake of his head.

The other man nodded. "Yes, Tony, there's a few answers to that question, Isn't there?"

Jaclyn frowned. "A few answers? I just want to find out where the information centre is, please."

"Well, miss. It depends on what information you want."

Another chuckle came from the man called Charlie. "If you want to know where to get a good cup of coffee, Tony here, is a connoisseur. He can direct you."

"And if you want to know whether to buy a pie at the bakery," Tony gestured to the bakery along the footpath, "or go to the Cyprus Café, there's really no right or wrong information. Isn't that a fact, Charlie?"

Charlie nodded. "If you want to know where any of the shops are, we can point you in the right direction too. You don't really need an information centre."

The frustration that had dogged Jaclyn since she had turned off the New England Highway and headed to Bindarra Creek resurfaced.

"You could almost say we are the information centre." The chuckle turned into a deep guffaw, and she bit back the sigh that threatened.

Again.

She pulled herself straight. "Thank you for your help. I'll ask in the newsagent."

"Sorry, love." Tony, the man with the pure white hair softened his expression. "What do you need to know? We don't actually have an information centre in Bindarra Creek. If we can't help you, the best place to go—if you're looking for someone—would be the post office."

"So you see, it really depends on what you need to know like we said," the other man interjected.

"Thank you." Jaclyn relented. After all the

whole town would know who she was within a few days. "I'm looking for somewhere to stay for a few days until I get settled in town."

"Settled? You're planning on staying here." This time the expression wasn't so soft as he looked at her city clothes.

"I'm the new school principal. I need to find somewhere to live."

"Well then, that I can certainly help you with. Come with me." Tony stood and crooked his arm. "I'll take you around to see Hunter. He runs the stock and station agency." His chest puffed out as he waited for her to take his arm. "My daughter actually owns it, and Hunter looks after it for her."

Charlie shuffled to his feet. "I'll come too. It's not far. Just around the corner next to the café."

Bemused and feeling a little bit like Alice in Wonderland, Jaclyn took his arm.

Chapter 4

"It's been a long day." Ryan yawned as he leaned back in the camp chair. "I'll have to hit the sack soon." Even though it was mid-spring, he'd lit the fire in the fire pit at the back of the house. He and Joe had been sitting beside the fire talking for hours. It was the best catch up they'd had for a few years—since Mum's funeral.

"Do you ever hear from Reg?" Joe asked curiously.

"Not for a long time. He used to ring me when he wanted money, but that stopped a few years back." Ryan picked up the bottle of port and topped up his glass.

"Just one for me before bed. I've got to drive early in the morning." Joe held his glass out and when Ryan had half-filled it, he raised it for a toast. "Here's to Mum."

"And to the memory of our camping days." Ryan clinked his glass with his brother's. It was one of the good memories and they were few and far between.

Reg, their stepfather, had been away shearing, and Mum had taken the two boys to the Warrumbungles. It had been just before she'd fallen ill, and they'd lost her by the Christmas of that year. The money that she'd hidden away from Reg for years had been enough to see Ryan off to uni to do his construction management degree the next year and had set Joe up to take to the shearing circuit.

"He's probably dead," Joe said.

"Drank himself into an early grave. I doubt if anyone would look for us to let us know," Ryan said.

"Unless he owed them money." Joe looked down at his glass. "We turned out okay despite him, didn't we?"

"Poor Mum had a tough few years though. I'll never forgive the old bastard for the way he treated her." Ryan tipped his head back and looked at the midnight sky brilliant with stars. There was no wind and the only sound apart from the crackling of the flames was the occasional low of a beast reaching them from the east paddock.

Life was good these days, so why did he feel so unsettled tonight?

"I'm going to get my swag out of the ute." Joe stood and put his hand over his mouth as he yawned too. "Okay if I come back on Friday and stay a couple more days? I've got to go over to Manilla and see a bloke about a contract, but I'll be back for the weekend. I've got a break between jobs."

"Mate, consider this a permanent base if you

want. I'd be happy to have some company." Ryan grinned. "And someone to help with the fencing if you're ever at a loose end."

"Great, I'll take you up on that."

"We'll head into town on the weekend too. I'm getting to know a few people and I've been asked to meet the volunteer rescue guys at the pub on Saturday afternoon. They'd probably appreciate having both of us."

Joe nodded. "I've heard they've done it tough out here over the past couple of years."

"Yeah, on top of the drought, Bindarra Creek's had its fair share of dramas. So, if there's any way I can help out in the community, I'm happy to pitch in."

Joe chuckled. "You've always been one of the good guys, haven't you, bro?"

Annoyance pricked at Ryan.

How many times had Reg taunted him about being Mr. Goody Two Shoes?

"Mum always taught us how important a community is. And honesty. I guess it's always been a part of me." He flicked a glance at his younger brother. "You, too, I hope."

Joe coloured. "I've had my silly times, but I've grown up now."

"I don't think I want to know about it." Ryan stood and took their dinner plates over to the small concrete tub that was at the back of the old farmhouse. He quickly rinsed the two plates and forks and left them on the side of the tub to dry. The barbeque could wait until the weekend to be cleaned. "I've got an early start tomorrow. I've got a tough meeting, and I want to check out some buildings before I go to the school."

"I'll leave before sun-up. Thanks for putting up with me."

Ryan smiled at his brother. "It's good to have you back."

##

It was still pitch black when the sound of Joe's ute starting up woke Ryan the next morning. He rolled over in his swag and thought of the day ahead. His appointment with Jaclyn was early afternoon, but he decided to go and have a closer look at the damaged building so that he had all the information at hand. Seeing Jaclyn at the school yesterday had given him a sleepless night.

Not only had he worried about the school buildings or that he'd be seeing a lot of her over the coming months—as the buildings were restored or demolished—but the memory of the times they'd spent together had tugged at his memory all night. He'd even dreamed about one of the concerts they'd been to in the Hunter Valley.

A crazy stupid dream. Jaclyn had been on the

gate selling tickets, and in his dream, she'd been hiding the money in her bag. The next minute she'd been up on the stage singing that old Abba song, *Money, Money, Money.*

Ryan sat up in bed and ran his hands over his face. Not enough sleep usually put him in a bad mood, and today he wanted to be on top of his game.

He'd cared about Jaclyn and thought they'd been close, but she'd avoided him after he'd told her she'd been too hard on that plumber. Every time he'd called, she'd been too busy to talk to him, and her voice had been distant. He'd seen her at a restaurant in the city a couple of weeks later with an older guy in a suit; maybe he'd been more suitable for what she wanted, more so than a building contractor whose dream was to live in the country.

Ryan shrugged as he made his way to the shower. He thought they'd been developing a relationship that could go further, but he'd obviously been a convenience to her. They had a professional relationship now, and he'd keep it that way. It didn't matter that Jaclyn Douglas had turned up in Bindarra Creek; Ryan had his farm and his goals were set. There would be plenty of other local girls who'd like to spend time in his company.

He didn't need a snobby school principal who valued money more than people.

So why the hell couldn't he get Jaclyn's face out
of his head as he stood beneath the hot water in the
makeshift shower?

***

The sun shining though the lace curtains woke
Jaclyn just before six the next morning. Despite
having a lot on her mind, she'd slept like a baby.
She closed her eyes again and burrowed into the
blissfully soft bed and feather pillow as she tried to
recall where she was.

As wakefulness pushed away the desire to keep
sleeping, the events of the day before came back to
her. Two kind gentlemen had taken her to the Stock
and Station Agency but there had been a closed sign
on the door. The white-haired gentleman had
suggested the Fig Tree Lodge and insisted on
calling the owner for her.

His smile had been wide as he'd turned to
Jaclyn in the street outside the Stock and Station
agency and held his thumb up. "Thanks, Edwina.
We'll bring her around now. Yes, Tony and I."
He'd paused as he listened to the other end of the
conversation, and Jaclyn sneaked a glance at her
watch when her stomach rumbled.

"I don't know," he said, before he turned to
Jaclyn and held the phone away from his ear.
"Sorry, dear, may I have your name for the

47

booking?"

"Douglas, Jaclyn Douglas."

She'd waited patiently as he repeated her name and then turned to her again. "And how long for, dear?"

Jaclyn bit her lip as she thought. "Until the end of the weekend please." By that time, she could scope out the town and find something more permanent. Maybe even something to buy.

"Excellent," Charlie said. "Come on, we'll take you there now."

Jaclyn looked longingly at the café next to the agency. The Cyprus Café—where Kellie had wanted them to have their meeting earlier—had a delicious smell wafting out from within and her stomach grumbled again.

"It's fine, thank you. Just give me the address and I'll drive there." Jaclyn looked at her watch again.

The man called Tony laughed and shook his head. "Fig Tree Lodge is only across the road from here, love." He pointed to the doctor's surgery directly across the road. "It's around the corner behind Dr Hargraves' surgery. About a one-minute walk. It's not far to anywhere in Bindarra Creek."

Heat ran into Jaclyn's cheeks when Tony gestured to her still grumbling stomach. "Once we get you set up with Edwina, there'll still be plenty of time for you to get something to eat."

"There's a pub with good food too. It's called the Riverside Pub and it's the other side of town. On the way to the bridge," Charlie said. "If the café's closed by the time you get settled you could always try there. Or there's the bowling club, and the rissole too."

"The Rissole?" she asked with a frown. "A restaurant?"

"The R.S.L. club, rissole for short. It has a bistro. Food's not bad," Tony said.

"Oh, okay. Thank you." Jaclyn had given in at their insistence, and they'd each taken an arm and escorted her–there was no other word for the solicitous way that they led her across the road— and as promised she was at the bed and breakfast within a minute or two.

A small woman with long gray hair was waiting inside the front gate.

"Thank you, gentlemen." She turned and held out her hand to Jaclyn. The woman's eyes were a dark hazel flecked with gold and her intense gaze held Jaclyn's eyes. Her grip was firm, and the smell of patchouli oil surrounded them.

"Welcome to Fig Tree Lodge. I'm Edwina Lette."

Jaclyn took the hand that was offered. "I'm Jaclyn Douglas."

The small woman put her head to the side in a curious bird-like movement. "Ah, the new principal. Welcome to Bindarra Creek."

"Thank you. Word gets around quickly." Jaclyn raised her eyebrows.

The woman's laugh was light. "When you have Kellie in your office, nothing's a secret." She tapped the side of her nose and then waved off the two men waiting on the footpath. "Off you go, you pair. I'll get Mrs. Douglas sorted."

"Please call me Jaclyn, and it's Ms." Jaclyn kept her tone light, although she was already feeling trapped. Control had been taken from her; all she'd wanted was a bed for the night, not an introduction to half the town. "Thank you again." She nodded to the two elderly men as they walked away with a wave from each of them.

The view of the house was obscured by the large Moreton Bay Figs in the centre of the lawn; there was just a small glimpse of white wrought iron lace edging a top veranda. The house came into sight at the side of a long gravel driveway that swept around the side.

"It's beautiful." Jaclyn drew a deep breath as they walked down the driveway towards the elegant building. Beautiful and colourful spring flowers filled garden beds along the edge of the drive and dotted the front lawn in random plantings in the shade of the big tree. A tyre swing hung from one of the tree branches.

Nostalgia tugged at Jaclyn. It reminded her of the childhood holidays she had spent with her maternal grandmother in the South Island of New Zealand. Gran's farm had been outside the small tourist town of Arrowtown, long before it had been made famous in the *Lord of the Rings* movies. She and Gran had spent every spring in the garden until Jaclyn had gone to boarding school on Sydney. It was her dream to have a place of her own like that one day. There was nothing like nurturing plants and watching them grow. Gran was in a nursing home in Alexandra, a small town near Queenstown, and Jaclyn was planning a trip over there in the long summer school holidays. They spoke on the phone each week, and although Gran was frail physically, she was still as sharp as a tack.

"It's been in my family since the town was settled," Edwina said, pride evident in her voice, but her eyes were shrewd, and Jaclyn felt uncomfortable beneath that steady gaze.

"And have you always lived here?"

"Most of my life." The older woman reached into her pocket and pulled out a small slip of paper. "This is the code to get into the lodge." She pointed to an electronic pad beside the front door. "I'm sure you're familiar with these types of things coming from the city."

Jaclyn nodded as Edwina put the code in and the door opened with a click.

"Welcome to Fig Tree Lodge. I've put you upstairs in the biggest room. We've been quieter than usual for a few months, but we're hoping that we'll get the spill-over from the hillbilly hoedown in summer."

"The hillbilly hoedown?" Jaclyn frowned and Edwina's laugh tinkled again.

"I'm not a fan of country music. The Country Music Festival is in Tamworth in January. Give me Led Zeppelin or Deep Purple any day." She reached out and took Jaclyn's hand. "Ah, not a fan of country music, either." Her eyebrows lifted and lessened the wrinkles on her face as her skin tightened and Jaclyn could see the once beautiful woman she must have been. "Jazz and blues, dear?"

Jaclyn pulled her hand back quickly as though it had been burned. "I beg your pardon?"

Edwina continued as though she hadn't spoken, and Jaclyn wondered if she'd heard correctly. "Even though we had some rain in the winter, it wasn't enough to break the drought, and it's not a very popular destination with the tourists at the moment. But things will look up, we have to always stay positive, don't we?"

Those shrewd eyes again had Jaclyn regretting

choosing to stay here. Not that she'd really chosen; she'd been railroaded by the two old men.

She nodded. "Yes. Of course."

Jaclyn followed Edwina into a timber-floored hall that ran down the centre of the house. Midway along the hall, stairs led to the upper floors. A hallstand held a bunch of sweet-smelling roses, and beeswax polish blended with it to provide a welcoming fragrance.

"That's the library to the left. Feel free to come down and use it. There's many books in there, something for all tastes."

When they reached the bottom of the staircase, Edwina pointed to the door across the hall. "That's the dining room. Breakfast will start at 6.30am. To make it easier for Lou to prepare, would you like a cooked breakfast or a continental?"

"I won't need breakfast but thank you."

This time the lips were prim. "I think you do. Breakfast is the most important meal of the day. As a teacher you should know that. Doesn't the best learning occur in the first two hours of the day? Don't schools have breakfast clubs to ensure that their students are fed and ready for learning?"

Jaclyn nodded slowly. "That's correct."

"We'll see you at 6.30. Would you like cereal and fruit, or eggs?"

"Cereal and fruit would be good. Thank you."

Jaclyn couldn't believe that she had agreed. Coffee, strong and black—had been her breakfast of choice over the past months.

"I might even come down and have breakfast with you, I think we need to get to know each other." Edwina walked to the staircase. "Come this way. I'll take you to your room."

Now Jaclyn lay in the soft bed watching the morning light play over the ceiling. After Edwina had shown her to her room, she'd walked back and brought her car over and parked on the road outside. A very quiet dinner at the RSL club–on Edwina's recommendation—and then an early night had ended Jaclyn's first night in her new town. One day down. Nine hundred and something to go.

The day loomed ahead, and her stomach tightened. She had an office to get into order, she had to meet the staff—perhaps call an assembly and introduce herself to the students, and then meet with Ryan Rossiter after lunch.

Climbing out of bed reluctantly, Jaclyn headed for the shower in the beautifully restored bathroom, refusing to look at the large and tempting claw-footed bath that sat beneath the window—that could be tonight's treat. She'd remember to buy some bubble bath and a bottle of wine on the way home from school.

After the day ahead, she was sure she'd need it.

"Good morning. I've set the table beneath the window for you." A solidly built woman with short blonde hair greeted Jaclyn as she walked into the dining room shortly after six-thirty.

"Thank you." Jaclyn smoothed her hands down her slim-fitting navy trousers before she took the seat at the table by the window. The woman disappeared into a room where morning radio provided a muted background noise. She picked up the serviette and unfolded it nervously on her lap. She would have been much happier having her usual black coffee, but who knew what would be open in a town this small on her way to school. As Jaclyn sat there waiting, her nose twitched as the aroma of freshly brewed coffee drifted in. Shortly after the woman returned and placed a bowl of bircher muesli and a bowl of fruit salad on the table.

"Edwina said you would be a muesli breakfast." The woman hovered at the table until the silence became uncomfortable. "I'm Lou. If there's anything else you'd like, let me know because I have to go and get my kids and husband out of bed. I don't want to be late for the training session at the SES this morning."

Jaclyn widened her eyes. "Am I the only one in for breakfast?"

Lou nodded. "Yes, but Edwina is going to join

you shortly.”

“I’m sorry. You didn’t need to come in just for me.”

Lou waved a dismissive hand. “It’s fine. It’s my job now, and we live in the old stables on the grounds, so no problem. Besides you wouldn’t get decent coffee anywhere in town before eight o’clock, and Edwina said you love your coffee, and that you’d be at school by then anyway.”

Jaclyn bit back her rising temper.

Did she just? Calm. Be calm. The day ahead was going to be hard enough.

“Thank you. I appreciate your—and Edwina’s—kindness.”

Lou shook her head. “Look I can see you’re uncomfortable, but this is Edwina’s house—and her way—and this is Bindarra Creek. It’s very different to the city, but hell, we all look out for each other, and if that means that the new school principal gets a decent breakfast, just take it in the spirit intended.” Her laugh was gruff. “And pay your bill when you check out.”

Jaclyn was lost for words and nodded as she looked up at the cook. “Thank you, and I will.”

Lou leaned forward and her voice was quiet. “You’ve come to a good place. Accept the help that comes your way. It looks tough on the outside, but trust me, there’s some very good people in this town. I know that well." She straightened and folded her arms. "Now, how do you take your coffee?"

"Black please."

Lou nodded and Jaclyn picked up her spoon as the cook disappeared into the kitchen. She had almost finished the muesli and fruit when the door to the hallway opened and Edwina walked in. If it hadn't been for the grey hair, and the wrinkled face, her clothes would have her mistaken for a much younger woman. Bright purple pants were topped with a yellow loose-fitting top, matched by the purple and yellow-striped head band that held her long hair back from her face.

"Namaste." After a light bow and her palms pressed together, Edwina dropped her hands and pulled out the chair opposite.

"Good morning, Edwina. You're about early." Jaclyn nodded her thanks as Lou crossed to the table and placed a large mug of coffee in front of her. She closed her eyes and inhaled.

"I have an early appointment today." Edwina was smiling at her when Jaclyn opened her eyes. "I used to love my coffee too, but at my age it keeps me awake all night and running off to the loo every fifteen minutes. Some of the CWA girls tell me to get those special pants, but I'm not old enough for them yet!" Her laugh was deep and husky, and

Jaclyn couldn't help but smile back.

Jaclyn wondered what Edwina's appointment was but thought it would be rude to ask. She was a private person and respected the same in others, but Edwina obviously sensed her curiosity.

"I've got a room at the back of the hairdresser. It's not far to walk there and it fills my day. I had a bit of a turn a while back and the family don't like me driving. Ridiculous," she muttered.

"What do you do there?"

"When it's time for you to know, I'll tell you. I think you need to come and see me," was the enigmatic reply. "But you need to settle into town and the school first."

Jaclyn nodded, unsure of what to say to that. "I must get moving. I want to get an early start. Is it okay if I take the coffee up to my room?"

"Of course, it is." Edwina gestured to Lou. "I'll have my chamomile tea now. You have a good day, Jaclyn."

Chapter 5

Jaclyn chose her outfit for the first day carefully. She wanted to look professional as she would be meeting the staff and students but was also aware that she would be cleaning out the mess in her office first. She chose a pair of navy tailored trousers, a loose white shirt, a waist length jacket and a red scarf. Standing in front of the oval mirror in the beautiful cedar antique dressing table, she pulled her hair back into a twist at the back of her head. A quick swipe of lip gloss and slipping into a pair of flat red pumps and she was ready for her first day at school.

Kellie had reluctantly issued her with school keys before she'd left yesterday afternoon. As Jaclyn had expected the car park was empty and she pulled into the space that was marked Principal. There were a couple of other cars at the end of the car park and she guessed they would be the cleaners' cars.

Another hurdle to be faced; she'd experienced her fair share of difficult cleaners, who liked to think they were a font of advice and knew as much about the politics of a school as the teaching staff. Jaclyn grinned ruefully; they often did. In a small community like Bindarra Creek they would be locals too, so she would have to tread carefully.

The main door and then the office door opened at the first turn of the master key, and she was pleased to smell a fresher smell in there than yesterday. The sweet fragrance of lavender surrounded her; there was one of those electronic room fresheners plugged into the power point next to the desk.

However, that was the only thing that had been attended to, but she had to be grateful for small mercies. Walking back into the main office, she spied a large bin and took it back into her office. Within ten minutes it was half full; empty coffee cups, a stack of crumpled paper bags that had filled the top drawer of the desk—along with a lot of crumbs—and a variety of paper rubbish from the top shelf of the first cupboard she opened.

Jaclyn sighed and closed the cupboard after clearing one shelf; at least if she could get the office looking tidy, she would look professional for any appointments she may have today. The interior of the cupboards could wait until the weekend. Reaching down to retrieve the overflowing bin from beneath the desk her eyes widened. She crouched down and peered into the darkness beneath the desk. The modesty board at the front of the desk had hidden the contents from her view from the other side. With a disgusted huff, she crawled beneath the desk and began pulling out the three pairs of men's shoes and socks—worn socks—that were beneath the desk.

She couldn't reach the last pair and stretched out on her stomach to reach them.

"Hello?" A tap on the door and a deep voice had her sitting up suddenly and she bumped her head on the edge of the desk on the way up.

Gripping the edge of the desk with one hand and holding a shoe and two socks with the other, she pulled herself to her feet to meet the amused eyes of Ryan Rossiter.

Oh, how embarrassing.

"Good morning, Ms Douglas." Ryan's lips twitched as he obviously fought back a smile.

Jaclyn waved her free hand and dropped the shoe and socks into the large bin. "Go on, you can smile. It's not often you find a principal on the floor beneath their desk with a handful of,"—she grimaced and lifted the socks between two fingers—"smelly socks."

"Not unless they've had a bad day, but it's a bit early for that." Ryan lifted his hands and for the first time, Jaclyn noticed that he held two takeaway coffee cups. "I won't take up your time now, I know our appointment isn't until after lunch, but I saw your car here when I came into town." He held up one coffee. "Still the same? Black? No sugar?"

Jaclyn nodded. "Thank you."

"I also have an ulterior motive. Before I head into the regional office, I'd like to have another look at the buildings. Do I have your permission to go on site this morning?"

Their fingers brushed as Ryan passed the coffee and a tingling jolt ran up Jaclyn's arm.

With a single nod, she stepped back. "I guess so. Thank you for the coffee. I'll see you at two o'clock."

Ryan held her gaze for a little bit too long for comfort, and Jaclyn was the first to look away.

"I hope you have a good first day at the school. It's very different to what you're used to, Jac."

She let the diminutive of her name pass. It was too early in the morning to start an argument. "I'm very aware of that. But don't worry. I'll cope. I'll see you this afternoon. At two. Thanks for the coffee."

"My pleasure and I'm sure you'll cope. I'll see you then." Ryan turned swiftly and was out the door before she could blink. She was pleased he'd called in; it seemed to have broken the ice between them a bit.

***

The sight of Jaclyn's shapely derriere poking out beneath her desk had been a fine start to the day.

Her mellow mood had been even better; for a moment it had been the Jac of old. Ryan knew that he made her nervous, and he wasn't sure how he felt about that. He took a swig of coffee as he headed towards the damaged high school building and cursed when he burnt his tongue. "Shit."

"Watch the language, buddy." The husky smoker tones reached him at the same time as the cigarette smoke did.

He walked into the hall where the two cleaners were sitting on the steps below the stage having a cigarette break. "Not a wise move, Helen. The new boss is in her office."

The school cleaner shrugged, and then coughed. "I'll put it out if I hear her coming. Once I finish this I'll go and say hello. I think she's got her hands full in that office. I didn't touch it last night because Dave made no effort to leave it nice for her. God, he turned it into a pig sty in the two weeks he was in there. I was going to do it this morning but sounds like she beat me to it. It'll be a change to have a boss who arrives with the cleaners. The best I could do was put an air freshener in there last night. Talk about stink. I've never smelled such bad feet on a man." Again, the husky laugh. "And I've had a few leave their shoes under my bed."

Ryan shook his head. "You're incorrigible, Helen."

"So, what's she like? Kellie didn't seem too impressed yesterday. Said she's a bit la-de-da." Helen shook her head and put her cigarette butt into a juice bottle that was on the floor beside her. "The community think we'd be better off with a bloke. Kev did a good enough job here and a lot of the old school don't think it's right to have a woman in charge. They were hoping that Dave stepped up, but you know what? He's lazy. I think it's good that she got the job, even if she is from the city and comes under a cloud. It'll be a breath of fresh air in the place."

Ryan let the mixed metaphors slip by. He wasn't sure what Helen meant by 'under a cloud'. But he wasn't going to let on that he already knew Jaclyn, and they had a past history. Unless she mentioned it to anyone, he wasn't going to say anything and he felt uncomfortable being a part of a gossip session, so he kept his reply brief. "I'm sure the department has appointed the best person to the job. Anyway, gals, have a good day. I have work to do."

He walked across to the building that still had blue and white police tape around it. The strong August westerlies had left some of the tape hanging in tatters, and it was easy to make his way into the charred building. Ryan had called into the fire station one Friday afternoon when he'd come to his property for the weekend a couple of weeks ago.

Kel Jones, the fire captain, had told him that the Education Department had already been considering demolition before the fire but there had been community opposition to that.

"It's not heritage listed," he said. "But it's one of the original buildings in the town. The arsonist started the fire in the garbage bins, and we got it under control before it spread out of the first room. I don't think there was much structural damage, it was mainly smoke and water that did the damage, but I guess as the assessor that's up to you."

"I wish." Ryan raised his voice over the loud voices in the bar. Kel had invited him to join him for a beer and the Friday afternoon Riverside Pub crowd was loud.

"What do you mean? It'll be quieter out the back." Kel gestured towards the beer garden and they walked out together.

"It's all down to the pencil pushers who hold the purse strings. If they think they can save a dollar demolishing the building and putting up a new one, that's what will happen."

"The community will fight that. They were already banding together before the fire. The school, particularly that building, is a part of the history of the town." Kel put his beer down on a vacant table overlooking the sluggishly flowing brown river. "Sorry, I know you have a job to do. If you were a local, you'd understand."

"I get what you're saying." Ryan nodded. "I grew up in Werris Creek and the community was strong there and pulled together to face all sorts of adversity." With a grin, he lifted his beer. "And I am going to be a local. I've just settled on my own property. Rossiter's Run out on the Tamworth Road."

Kel picked up his glass and clinked it against Ryan's. "That's great news, mate. There's good land over in the foothills of the Great Divide, you'll get a bit more rain than we do in town. It's good to have new people moving out here. Young people. Give some thought to joining the SES; they do a great job and have a social occasion every so often. It's a good way to become a part of the town quickly." He looked across the beer garden; it was filling up. "If you need any advice or a hand, there's plenty around to help out. Have you met Jon and Cleo Kendall? They're probably your closest neighbours. I saw them in the bistro when we came in."

Ryan thought back to that night in the pub as he walked into the building. He'd met the Kendalls— and a few other locals—and had been made to feel very welcome. It had cemented his certainty that Bindarra Creek was a good place to settle. Just like where he'd grown up.

He took his time looking at the building and by the time he headed back to his ute, the car park was full, and he couldn't help wondering how Jaclyn was faring.

He shook his head as he backed out of the car park and headed for Tamworth.

Not your problem.

But he did wonder why there were so many cars parked along the road outside the high school.

Chapter 6

"What did I do to deserve this?" Jaclyn closed her office door just before two and crossed to the desk, sat down and put her head in her hands. At least she'd finished cleaning up the room before the office manager had appeared in the doorway just before eight-thirty this morning.

Maybe she *should* have taken the option of being demoted to a large school in the city, rather than taking an appointment as principal to a smaller school in the country, but Jaclyn knew she had done nothing wrong and refused to take up that option. At least in the city she knew how things worked. Procedures should be the same here too, but there was a distinct lack of structure and when she'd asked Lea, the office manager, for the policy and procedures booklet, she'd been met with a blank stare.

Lea Kendall, the office manager, was a tall woman with rounded shoulders and an unwelcoming demeanour. Her thin blonde hair was permed in the old-fashioned style where you could see the rows where the rollers had been.

Jaclyn wasn't sure how long Lea had been standing at the door watching her as she wiped down the shelves behind her desk with paper towel and some cleaning spray she'd found in the kitchen cupboard. A movement had caught Jaclyn's eye and when she looked over, Lea was standing there, arms folded and a frown wrinkling her forehead. She stepped into the room, and her arms remained folded across her chest.

"There's no need for you to do that. I could have got the cleaners in."

Jaclyn bit back the response that sprung to her lips to ask "well, why didn't you?" Her immediate impression was that her office manager was not going to be an ally.

She refused to give into the sigh that rose and took in a calming breath. The first essential for a principal is a loyal and efficient office manager.

Although to be fair, she knew she had to win that trust, but these first signs were not encouraging. She picked up the roll of paper towel, wiped her hands and walked across with her hand held out.

"You must be Lea. I'm Jaclyn. It's good to meet you."

Her outstretched hand was ignored, but she was given a terse nod.

Yep, she'd picked it.

"Where do you want Dave to go? He was going to go to the staffroom, but it's long way for us to send students to the Deputy."

"I was under the impression that David was

Acting Deputy before he stepped up?"

"Yes, that's right."

Jaclyn silently counted to five and smiled sweetly. "For the time being, he can go back to the staffroom. I'll have a meeting with the school executive after school today and we'll work all those things out."

"After school? I don't think so."

Jaclyn raised her eyebrows. "What afternoon is the executive meeting usually held?"

"We haven't had one since Kevin left last month. There's no need. Everyone knows their job."

"I will have to disagree with you there." Jaclyn kept her voice even. "I'd appreciate it, Lea, if you could notify the senior executive that we'll meet this afternoon. And yourself, of course, as the senior administration manager."

Lea shrugged. "I'll tell them. I can't promise that anyone will come, and I have to go home at three today, so I won't be there."

"Very well. I'll meet the staff at recess. Would you please let everyone know to come to the staff room for morning tea? Kellie mentioned a cake yesterday. If you'd like to send her up to the bakery, I'll give you some money so there's enough morning tea for all the staff."

Lea shook her head. "There's no point. No one comes to the staff room. They all stay in their own rooms. If you want to meet them, you'll have to go to the staffrooms."

Before Jaclyn could reply, the woman turned to the door. "I have to go and open the office window. It's eight-thirty."

Jaclyn was left standing there with her mouth open. She closed it and crossed to the desk and sat down. She was going to have to pull out her best managerial skills by the look of things. Without rocking the boat too much, the first action would be a closed-door meeting with her manager.

##

By the time the bell went for recess, Jaclyn's mood had deteriorated so much, for one brief moment she'd even considered getting in her Audi and driving back to Sydney. Her main worry for the day—the meeting with Ryan—had been pushed to the back of her thoughts as a stream of people inundated her office.

As soon as she'd sat at her desk when Lea left the room, a small woman with curly grey hair walked in and sat down opposite Jaclyn.

"G'day, love. How's it going?"

Jaclyn frowned and glanced at the logo on the polo shirt. "I'm sorry, Lea didn't tell me you were waiting for an appointment."

The woman's laugh was husky and turned into a cough. "Nah, I didn't have an appointment, I just called in to say hello and to tell you that the three toilets in the high school girls' block are overflowing. You'll have to get a plumber in, but I don't like your chances today." She reached over the desk and held her hand out.

Jaclyn half-stood and her hand was shaken in a firm grip.

"I'm Helen, Helen Bateman. Head cleaner." She sat up straight in the chair and smiled. "Except for old Curly, I've been here at Bindarra Creek longer than anyone. In the primary or the high schools. If you want to know anything that's going on in the school—or town—you give me a hoy and I'll fill you in." Jaclyn's eyes widened as the cleaner winked at her, but she managed a nod.

"Thanks for stopping by to say hello, Helen, and I'll keep that in mind."

The cleaner lowered her voice. "You won't survive here long if you don't listen. There's already a lot of talk about why you left Sydney to come here, so you take care, love. It's good to have a woman run the show. About bloody time."

A cold chill settled in Jaclyn's chest and for a moment she thought she was going to faint.

No!

The director had assured her that her situation was totally confidential. If word had got this far out, it explained the cold reception she'd received from the office manager.

The morning had declined from that point on, and a headache began to build behind Jaclyn's temples. It appeared that there was no need for appointments in this school—and the steady stream of parents, community, and teachers who appeared in her doorway, came in and then sat in front of the desk without an invitation, had Jaclyn shaking her head.

Why was she here? What did she think of the community? What were her thoughts on the drought? Did she believe in accountability for teachers? Did she have the authority to give pay rises? Are the buildings going to be restored?

At two o'clock when Lea finally did tap on the door—some progress—and announced that her two o'clock appointment was here, Jaclyn was exhausted.

She had honestly been hit with every question that was possible. And nonstop, with no appointment or calling in at the front office. It appeared that they were used to walking down the corridor and entering the principal's office without being invited.

From tomorrow, things would be very different.

She looked up with a smile as Lea ushered Ryan into the room.

"Shut the door please, Lea, and there are to be no interruptions please."

The look Lea shot in her direction was curious as Ryan put another takeaway coffee cup on the table.

Jaclyn could have hugged him but restrained herself.

"Thanks for seeing me on your first, day, um, Jaclyn." His voice was careful, and Jaclyn relaxed in her chair.

"Thanks for providing me with coffee twice today. It's honestly been a lifesaver." She shook her head. "I feel as though I've been here a week."

Ryan's grin sent a familiar warmth down low in her belly. "A typical day in the life of a school principal?"

Jaclyn nodded and picked up her coffee. "You could say that. This is lunch." She gestured to the cup she was holding.

"Would you like to go out and have a proper meal after we do the inspection together? We could talk over a sandwich. I know how you need to eat." Ryan's frown was sympathetic, but Jaclyn shook her head.

"No, I'll be fine. I think it would be better to be available for the rest of the afternoon. I haven't had a chance to have a talk with my relieving predecessor yet or any of the head teachers. It's been a busy morning. Or been introduced to the students at an assembly." She folded her hands in her lap and held his gaze, ignoring the attraction that flared in her. "I'm sorry, Ryan. I haven't had a chance to look at any of the property files yet."

"I've been over at Regional Office and Warren Greenup said he'd emailed them to you."

She shook her head. "He may have done, but I have no access to the computer or the Department portal yet. I haven't had a chance to catch up with the computer person at the school."

She closed her eyes and took a deep breath, as she wondered how much to tell Ryan. He was going out of his way to be kind.

He deserved the truth.

Chapter 7

Ryan watched as Jaclyn closed her eyes. Her fair skin was pale, and there were dark shadows beneath her eyes. For the first time he noticed a couple of fine wrinkles at the corner of her eyes. They hadn't been there a few months ago. She opened her deep green eyes and they held his as she took another deep breath.

"Ryan? I want to tell you—"

They both jumped as the door flew open and banged against the wall. Dave stood there.

"We need you outside. That bastard of a Parch kid has lit a fire underneath the kindergarten classroom, and we need an ambulance because he threw a brick at Mandy Kaminsky when she called out to him, and it hit the kid she was with, and she's out cold."

Jaclyn jumped to her feet, picked up the phone and pressed the intercom button "Lea, call an ambulance and the fire brigade. Now."

Ryan stood and followed Jaclyn and Dave as they hurried down the corridor.

"The ambulance is on the way. Where will we send it? What's happened?" Lea's face was pale.

"David?" Jaclyn deferred to the deputy.

"Send it to the kindergarten block," Dave replied. "Mandy is with Selina."

"Lea, can you call the child's parents and let them know we've called for medical assistance," she called as they passed the front office.

Lea hurried to the phone and Ryan caught up to Jaclyn as she pushed open the main door. "You'll have to show me where the kindergarten block is please, David."

"I'll come with you, in case you need some more help," Ryan said.

"Thank you." Jaclyn's voice was calm as they both hurried to keep up with Dave.

"That's the kindergarten room, and there's that bastard kid," the deputy yelled.

"Please watch your language, David." Jaclyn headed for the building. "Ryan, can you help him stop that boy. It looks like he's trying to light the leaves near that other room."

The boy looked up and spotted the trio and dropped the can he was holding and took off towards the school oval. As Ryan started running towards him, he called out to Jaclyn.

"Get the kids out of that room, there's smoke coming from underneath it."

The sound of sirens filled the air as Ryan and Dave ran after the boy who had already reached the back of the school. Ryan passed Dave and looked ahead. The boy was coming to the high brick fence behind the primary classrooms.

Ryan quickly glanced to the right and saw there was only one way and chased after the boy. Ryan reached the gate and turned, just in time to see the kid shinny up the sheer brick wall and disappear over the top. He took off and headed towards the other side of the fence but by the time he reached it there was no sign of anyone.

Dave was waiting at the gate.

"How did he get over that fence?" Ryan asked.

"Slippery little tyke has form. It doesn't matter," Dave said. "We know who it is. It's that Parch kid; he's trouble with a capital T. Should have been expelled months ago. The do- gooder welfare people from the regional office said he comes from a difficult background, so we have to give him a chance. I'll give him a bloody chance when I get hold of him."

Ryan bent over and took a few deep breaths. It had been a while since he'd sprinted like that. "Come on, we'll go and see if we can help out back there."

The ambulance and the fire truck were parked near the kindergarten building

As Ryan and Dave reached the kindergarten block, the paramedics carried a stretcher out. Jaclyn was standing at the door; her lips were pursed, and she was tapping one finger nervously against the side of her skirt. She looked up as they approached.

"The little bastard got away," Dave said.

Jaclyn's forehead creased in a frown and she stepped forward and took the deputy's arm. "A word please, David. Come over here with me."

Ryan stepped away and watched as the ambulance drove out slowly, but he could still hear Jaclyn's terse voice as she reprimanded Dave for his language.

"Unprofessional . . . inappropriate . . ." Her words carried over to Ryan and he moved further away. Sympathy rose in him for both Dave and Jaclyn. Dave was getting carpeted, but it was an awful way for Jaclyn to be introduced to a new school. A critical incident with an injured student, not to mention the fire being checked by the firemen who were now walking around the adjacent building.

Jaclyn was hard and he had no doubt she could handle the situation.

Ryan shook his head. No matter why she was here, no one deserved a first day like this.

***

When Jaclyn finished talking to David—who foolishly had made the mistake of arguing with her—her heart rate was up, and her hands were shaking. She swallowed and took a deep breath; this was *not* the time to have a panic attack. Looking over towards the building where the fire truck was parked, she caught sight of a man in uniform heading her way. He stopped and spoke briefly to Ryan who was across the quadrangle. He walked across to Jaclyn with the fireman.

"Ms Douglas, this is Kel Jones, the fire chief. Kel, Jaclyn Douglas."

Jaclyn held her hand out and it was engulfed in a large and firm grip. "I'm pleased to meet you, Ms Douglas. I'm sorry it was under these circumstances, and on your first day here, I believe?"

She nodded and forced a rueful smile. "That's correct. But unfortunately, these things happen in schools."

"The leaves didn't catch fire, but we've confiscated the can of mower fuel that he left there. My boys are underneath the kindergarten room now, but it looks like that fire didn't take either, so we should be able to get this truck out of the way before the end of school. It must be getting close now."

Jaclyn glanced down at her watch. It was already a quarter to three. "I'm sorry, I'm not familiar with the bell times yet, but I imagine it will be around three."

A soft voice came from behind her. "The

primary bell rings at three, and the high school at three-fifteen."

Jaclyn turned. A pretty young woman with a round face and short curly brown hair was standing behind her. It was the woman who'd come into the office with the student when she'd been waiting yesterday afternoon.

"I'm Mandy Kaminsky," she said, and her voice shook a little this time. "I'm Selina's aide. I shouldn't have called out to Terry. If I hadn't Selina wouldn't have got hit with the brick. I feel dreadful. It was all my fault."

Jaclyn took Mandy's arm and glanced across at Kel and Ryan. "Don't be silly, Mandy. You did the right thing. It's not your fault at all. By calling out to him, you could have saved the kindergarten room catching fire and then we would have had a fleet of ambulances here."

Tears welled in the young woman's eyes. "Really? I won't lose my job? I'm only casual and part-time."

"Of course not. Now why don't we all go over to the office and I'll get Lea to make you a cup of tea." She kept hold of Mandy's arm; the young woman's face was very pale.

"Gentlemen." Jaclyn looked around, but David had disappeared. Ryan and Kel were the only ones standing there. "Come back to my office and we'll debrief."

"I'll go and check that everything's alright, and then I'll come over. I'll be there in a few minutes," Kel said.

"I'll make another appointment to do the site inspection with you, Jac—Ms Douglas," Ryan said.

Jaclyn shook her head. "No. We'll do it this afternoon. Or do you have another appointment?"

Ryan's eyes crinkled as he grinned. "Only with a few cattle and they'll be happy to wait. If you're sure?"

"Yes, you had an appointment and we'll keep it. It might be a bit late, but we'll have time after school."

She glanced from Ryan to Mandy. "Perhaps you could take Mandy for a coffee and keep an eye on her while I talk to the fire chief."

The young woman shook her head. "Oh, no I'm fine. I was just a bit shook up."

"Come on, Mandy, I could do with a coffee. It'll be company for me while I wait for my appointment with Ms Douglas." Ryan smiled at the young woman, and Jaclyn remembered what a kind man he was. In the time they'd been seeing each other, she'd seen his kindness and concern for others often. She stared over his shoulder; if anyone had needed help when he was around, he was the first to offer. Shame he hadn't been there for her when she'd needed support.

Jaclyn straightened her back as Mandy nodded and Ryan held out his arm. The pang of something—not jealousy, she told herself— as Mandy took it and they walked away together made her cross. She tried to focus on the situation at hand as she headed back to the administration block.

Lea was standing there with a scowl. "You've got three people waiting for you in your office. And Mr Parch is not happy that he had to wait."

Jaclyn firmed her voice. "I'm going to go down to the kitchen while you go in and make an appointment for each of them." She raised an eyebrow. "I assume it is three individual matters? Ask Mr Parch to wait in the foyer until I am ready to see him and please ask the others to make a time for tomorrow."

Lea's tone was stubborn. "That's not how we do things here."

"Well, Lea, you and I need to have a meeting tomorrow because that is how we will be doing things here from now on." Jaclyn stared at the woman until she looked down. "I know it's been a busy day, but I'd like you to do one more thing for me before you leave this afternoon."

"I have to go in five minutes," was the sullen reply.

"What time do you usually work until? Are you

taking leave this afternoon?" If her office manager could be uncooperative, she could be reminded of her working hours.

Lea's cheeks filled with colour. "You might think I'm slack leaving early, but I'm usually here at least until five-thirty every day." Her voice shook. "My husband has a medical appointment this afternoon and he can't drive himself.

"That's not a problem, but could you please use that five minutes to either call the computer coordinator for me or give me their name and extension. I need to get onto the school network to check my email and set up a shared diary for appointments with you." Jaclyn softened her voice. "It's the best way for both of us and we'll operate much more efficiently that way."

Lea nodded. "I'll call Craig Sanders. He's the year six teacher and gets a time allowance to look after the computer stuff."

"Thank you. I'll see you tomorrow. Please book in for the first appointment with me. I've got a few questions about the school, some procedures and the finances, that I'd hoped we could discuss today." Jaclyn lightened her tone with a chuckle. "Poor Mandy had to tell me what time the bell went."

As she spoke, the bell rang. "Just do those two jobs for me, please, Lea, and I'll see you tomorrow. I hope your husband is all right."

Jaclyn headed for the small kitchen at the end of the corridor and flicked the kettle on.

She stood there gripping the worktop with tense fingers.

What have I done? Was this school going to be another failing point in her career?

Jaclyn blinked away the tears that threatened and squared her shoulders.

She would be strong. After the interview with Terry Parch's father, she had to meet with Ryan.

Chapter 8

Ryan left Mandy at the café as soon as they had finished their coffee. The young woman had listened to him and accepted that the incident wasn't her fault; Ryan was keen to get back to the school for his meeting with Jaclyn. He'd been surprised that she wanted to have it today, but it suited him. The only problem was it meant that the cattle work he'd scheduled for this afternoon wasn't going to happen. He had the first meeting at the SES tomorrow, and then next week he had visits to schools at Gunnedah and Boggabri. The area that he was responsible for meant a lot of time on the road. He'd leave his ute in Tamworth and take a government car from the compound to travel further west.

Ryan had offered to drop Mandy home, but she waved him off. "Thanks, but I'm going to talk to Thalia for a while, and then I've got a fire and rescue meeting." She looked up at him from beneath her lashes and her cheeks were pink. "You should join us."

"I'm going to."

Mandy's cheeks went a deeper pink. Ryan paid

for their coffees and jumped in his ute and drove back to the school. The school yard was deserted. The afternoon buses had all gone, and by the look of the car park—one black Audi alone—the staff had already left too.

The front door was unlocked, and he pushed it open and walked down the corridor before tapping on Jaclyn's open door. She was sitting at her desk looking at the computer screen, a frown marring her forehead.

She looked up, but he sensed a coolness in her voice. "I'm almost ready. I'm just looking at the last of the recommendations from state office."

Ryan waited by the door. "Recommendations? I haven't seen any of those."

"They came through from Sydney this afternoon."

"I haven't checked my email yet. I'll do it when I get home." He frowned. "Unless there's something that I need to know before we inspect the buildings together."

"No, the email listed some costings for replacement versus refurbishment."

"And?" he asked raising one eyebrow. He wasn't prepared to trust Jaclyn to do the right thing.

"And there's very little difference in the cost. However, they are pushing for demolition."

"And is that there in black and white or is it

your spin, Ms Douglas?"

"No, it is *not* my spin, Mr Rossiter. I am simply recounting what is in my email."

"Well, I suggest that we go out and have a close look at those building and I'll show you where I have assessed that restorative work can be done and solve the need for demolition. And just so you know, I've also had a few specialist tradesmen take a look—a plumber and an electrician—and they agree that it is all able to be restored."

Jaclyn was sitting straight staring at him, but he noted the twin spots of colour on her pale cheeks. She stood before he could take a seat. "We'll do the inspection now, and we can talk when I am in a more informed position."

He followed her down the corridor to the back door of the administration building.

"Oh, just a moment," she said. "I need to lock the front door before we go."

"I was going to mention that it was unlocked, and I was able to come straight in. It's not safe when you're in the school alone, Jac."

She looked at him over the top her sunglasses. "I'm aware of WHS regulations, Ryan, and yes, it was an oversight at the end of a stressful day."

He waited outside the back door, and she key-locked it as they went outside.

"The cleaners are on site, so technically I'm not

alone until they leave at six.”

“You’ll be gone by then, won’t you?” He raised his eyebrows as she joined him, and they began to walk down to the charred building.

This time her eyebrows raised as she slipped her sunglasses on. It was quite dim outside, and he wondered if she really needed them.

“After the day I’ve had, Ryan, I’ll be pleased if I’m home before ten o’clock.”

“Where are you staying?” he asked curiously. “The motel?”

She shook her head. “No. At a B and B.”

“Do they do dinner?”

“No, it’s a bed and *breakfast*.” He was sure Jaclyn rolled her eyes behind those designer sunglasses.

“Now, don’t snap my head off, this is merely a professional invitation, not personal.” Ryan glanced at his watch. “It’s already after five. Why don’t we look at the building and then we can discuss it over dinner?”

She bit her lip as he waited for a response. “Where?”

“I’ve only arrived here recently, but I know they do a good meal at the pub near the river, and the RSL. The bowling club’s the closest to here, but I’m pretty sure they only open Friday and Saturday nights for meals. What do you say? You have to eat, and the IGA closes at five thirty."

"Thank you. As you say, I have to eat, and we can make it a business meeting."

"Good."

They reached the building and Ryan lifted the blue and white tape for Jaclyn to step beneath it.

"The building was boarded up before the fire in August, and Kel jemmied it off once the fire was under control. So the damage around the windows is from that, not any building degradation or the fire itself."

Jaclyn nodded and slipped her sunglasses off and tucked them into the pocket of her jacket. It was quite dark inside, but there was still enough light to see.

"The original building was made up of five classrooms, and the rooms are very big." Ryan pointed up as they stood in the first doorway. "What I'd like to see is have these rooms turned into specialist rooms, technology rooms—woodwork and metalwork. The students have been without adequate facilities for a long time and the VET students have been bussed into Tamworth once a week, ever since the senior students started again at the beginning of this year. It's only a small cohort here now, but the kids were bussing it to Tamworth or boarding at Armidale. It's hard for them because most of them are from properties and with the drought and its firm grip, they're needed at home."

Jaclyn turned to him and he could see the surprise in her eyes. "I'm sorry to say it, but you know more about the school than I do, Ryan."

"I do my homework," he replied. It was hard to take his eyes from her face, and hard to reconcile this woman with the happy and loving person he'd shared a few weekends away with earlier in the year.

Don't go there.

There was a harder edge and a bitterness in her expression now that hadn't been there before, but Ryan knew Jaclyn well enough to see through to the vulnerability beneath that.

"As I do mine, as you well know. I'll be up front with you. I only found out on Monday that I was appointed to Bindarra Creek Central. I packed and spent Wednesday and half of yesterday on the road and arrived after lunch. I'm ashamed to say I know very little about the school, apart from the director's wish to have the buildings replaced."

"What happened at Sanctuary Gardens, Jac?"

She shook her head. "That's past history. I'm here to fulfill the department's brief, give my opinion on the buildings and then focus on building the school up to one that is respected."

Ryan let his curiosity go and pulled his phone from his pocket and turned on the flashlight app.

"Let me show you the building."

***

Jaclyn was impressed as Ryan took her on a thorough tour of the building. The smell of burnt timber still lingered and there were piles of ash in some corners. She stepped carefully over the tape that was around the main doorway and at one stage he held out his hand to help her step over a large block of fallen timber. She ignored the reaction of her nerve endings after the brief touch ended.

As much as Jaclyn hated to admit it, there was sense in Ryan's words; he'd given a lot of thought to the proposal to restore the old building. From her past knowledge of the way he worked, she knew his decisions were well thought out. He followed the best route and was well-respected in the department. From the little she'd seen of the town, she could understand that the community would feel strongly about the building not being demolished. By the time they stepped outside, she was having doubts about the feasibility of demolition.

Restoration was something she was going to have to investigate in depth, but she had trusted Ryan before, and her instincts were telling her to trust him again.

"Thank you, Ryan," she said quietly. "That was most informative. It gives me a lot to think about."

"Good. Are you happy to go for dinner now? On the department's account."

She nodded. "Thank you. I just have to get my bag from the office. I'll meet you in the car park."

Jaclyn went back to the office and collected her handbag and laptop. As she left, she glanced at her watch. It was just before six. The cleaners would set the alarms when they left shortly after the hour. She made a snap decision not to come back to the school. She had her laptop and could deal with the emails and paperwork from the room at Fig Tree Lodge. She had been able to pick up a Wi Fi connection there last night. She put her hand up to cover a yawn; tiredness tugged at her.

Maybe she shouldn't have agreed to dinner with Ryan. Maybe she should have picked up a takeaway and focused on her emails instead.

Life balance, Jackie dear. Gran's voice was as clear as if she'd been in the room with her. She nodded to herself. Today was the first day of at least three years in this school; she didn't have to solve all the problems in the first hour.

Locking the office door behind her, she glanced over to the car park. Helen—the cleaner—was next to Ryan engrossed in a deep conversation. It was a timely reminder to her that in his position, Ryan would have the ear of many people, both at the school, and in the community, and she had to make her own decisions and not be swayed by him.

With that in mind, she straightened, and was perhaps a little distant in her response to Helen when she spoke to her.

"G'day, boss. A busy day, I hear." The gravelly voice was followed by a husky cough.

Jaclyn nodded and then turned to Ryan. "I'll take my car and meet you there."

She regretted saying that as Helen perked up with interest.

"Do you know where the pub is?" Ryan asked.

Jaclyn shook her head and couldn't help acknowledging Helen's curious look. "A business meeting," she commented briefly, and then immediately regretted her need to explain.

"Follow me. It's not far away."

She nodded and headed to her car as Ryan waved to Helen.

The Riverside Hotel was on the other side of town and the streets were deserted. The only life she saw was a couple of teenagers riding push bikes with fishing roads attached to the back. Jaclyn indicated to turn right into the drive at the side of the pub and followed his car down to the car park. She was surprised to see it almost full and looked around carefully for a vacant spot where she wasn't parked too close to cars on either side.

She hitched her handbag onto her shoulder and

clicked the remote to lock the door just as Ryan
sauntered over.

"There were a couple of parks closer to the
pub," he commented. "Up where I parked."

She smiled. "I know but I'm a bit precious about
my car. I never park it in a supermarket car park
either."

"Wise move." He looked around at the car park
with a frown. "I'm just hoping that we'll get a table.
It's pretty crowded already."

Jaclyn walked beside him to a set of stairs at the
back entrance to the hotel. There was a covered area
that led down to a beer garden on the river side, and
it was quite crowded. Ryan forged a path through
the drinkers on the verandah, and Jaclyn followed
him inside. Apart from being in the country, it was
not very different to any of the establishments she
was used to in Sydney. Glasses clinking, animated
conversations, and men in work gear lining the front
bar. The familiar mix of spilt beer, oil from the deep
fryers in the bistro, and stale cigarette smoke—
absorbed for years by the timber walls of the pub in
the days before it was illegal to smoke in Aussie
hotels.

Ryan headed for the door with the bistro sign
above it in the front of the pub, and when he pushed
the door open, he turned to her with a relieved
smile.

"Plenty of empty tables. We're early enough to snag one near the window overlooking the river too." He picked up a couple of menus and gestured for her to precede him to the table.

Jaclyn sat, feeling a little overdressed in her work trousers and jacket. It was warmer inside so she slipped her jacket off and removed the scarf from around her neck. The white shirt was casual enough to fit in.

"Would you like a drink before we order? The usual?" Ryan tilted his head to the side and that unruly lock fell across his forehead. He lifted his hand and pushed it back as she'd seen him do dozens of times. His hair was in need of a cut. Jaclyn couldn't help smiling. In Sydney, Ryan had always been too busy to get a haircut, and it looked like nothing had changed. She straightened her back and sat up; reminiscing wasn't going to get her anywhere. This was a business meeting, no matter how nice he was being, or how cute he looked with that unruly lock of hair and those gorgeous eyelashes. Jaclyn focused on being strong—Gran had taught her to be thoughtful and to tell the truth, but look where being nice had gotten her.

"I think you probably deserve a wine after the afternoon you've had," Ryan's voice interrupted her thoughts.

She looked up and held his dark-eyed gaze.

"Just a small glass of white with a soda on the side. I have work to do tonight, and I'm driving. Thank you."

She watched as Ryan made his way across to the side bar that ran along the edge of the bistro counter. It wasn't long before a barman came and took his order, but he stayed there chatting for a few minutes after the drinks were poured. He walked back juggling the wine, the soda and a glass of Coke.

He sat down and picked up his glass. "I would have had a beer, but I have a fair drive home on country roads."

"You don't live in town?"

He shook his head. "No, I've bought a property out on the Tamworth Road."

"It's what you've always wanted, isn't it?"

"It is." Lifting his glass with a smile, Ryan waited for Jaclyn to pick up hers. "Anyway, cheers and congratulations on your appointment to Bindarra."

Jaclyn looked at him over the top of her glass as she touched her glass to his.

Was he being facetious, or did he really mean it?

"I must say I didn't expect it, but I hope you'll be happy here." His expression sobered. "It's a real coincidence us ending up in the same town after we—"

Jaclyn's face heated as he broke off.

"Anyway, Jac. I hope You're happy here and it's what you want.

Oh no, it wasn't at all what she wanted.

Tears pricked at Jaclyn's eyes as she wondered what she really did want. The dream job she'd aspired to and had achieved at Sanctuary Gardens had had a sting in the tail and look where she'd ended up.

Don't trust anyone.

Jaclyn reached down into her handbag to cover her distress and pulled out her phone.

She kept her voice crisp when she looked up. "So, let's talk buildings."

Before Ryan could answer her phone dinged with an incoming email. She glanced down and when she saw it was from Peter Hughes, she held her phone up. "Please excuse me for a moment, Ryan. I need to read this before we talk."

She quickly scanned the contents of the email and tried not to react as Ryan waited for her to read it.

Peter Hughes had been her deputy principal at Sanctuary Gardens and had also relieved in head office on a number of occasions. He had been her advocate when everything had gone pear-shaped at school, and from his email she learned he had also left the school and moved to Head Office on a permanent basis. He'd been a very focused executive member—and thus not well liked— and Jaclyn had to speak to him about micromanaging the staff a number of times.

A heads-up Jaclyn. I have been appointed to the Properties Office in town as a senior manager, and I'm overseeing regional works. I may be out of line here, but you need to know that the local properties office will tell you that a restoration is more viable financially, as they have their own agenda and budget to consider.

I know you have only just arrived at your new school, but please do not be conned into any of their cost-saving talks. It is essential that you follow protocol as you well know by your recent unfortunate experience. I would hate to see you be made a scapegoat again. I will call you on Monday with further updates.

Jaclyn slipped the phone into her handbag as confusion filled her. This was her first country appointment, but she hadn't expected that the Sydney office would have much say out here. The regional office was a substantial size with its own regional director and covered many schools—including Bindarra Creek Central. What did Peter mean by "be made a scapegoat"?

A muscle twisted in her stomach as she held her

breath. Nausea soon followed, and for a moment Jaclyn though she was going to be sick. She could *not* go through all of that again. She closed her eyes as she tried to compose herself.

"Everything okay?" Ryan asked.

She forced a smile to her face and was pleased when her voice came out in a normal tone. "Yes, all good. Just some admin stuff." She propped her chin in her hand and rested her elbow on the table; it helped to hold her head steady. Her whole body felt as though it was shaking. "Now can you take me from what we saw this afternoon, through to the finished vision for the buildings. Convince me that restoration is the best way to go."

"I can and I will. It's something, as I told you, that I feel very strongly about." Ryan's expression was intense along with his voice. "But let's order our meals first. If I start showing you the diagrams before we order, we'll get sidetracked. Have you had a chance to look at the menu yet?"

Jaclyn shook her head and picked it up. As she began to read, a young couple stopped at the table to talk to Ryan.

"Hello, Ryan. We seem to meet here all the time," the man said.

Jaclyn spotted a Thai salad listed and put the menu back on the table. She couldn't think of an excuse not to eat; her stomach was churning, but she could pick at a salad as they discussed the buildings.

"Hi, Jon. We do." Ryan chuckled. "Even though would you believe it's only the second time I've been in the Riverside pub! Jaclyn, this is Jon and Cleo Kendall. They're my neighbours." He gestured to Jaclyn. "Guys, Jaclyn is the new principal at the school."

"Hi," the woman said shyly. "Welcome to town, Jaclyn."

Jaclyn nodded. "Thank you."

"You can't have been here long?" Jon said. "It's only a couple of weeks since Kevin left."

"Just a couple of days," she said.

"How about we join you for a drink? We can tell you all you need to know about the town. Local knowledge. Cleo and I grew up here," Jon said. "And you would have met my mother. She's the office manager at the school."

"Oh." Anxiety continued to tug at Jaclyn. She shouldn't have come. She should have insisted that she and Ryan had their meeting in her office and then she could have stayed there to work. The last thing she wanted to do was get involved in social chit chat; there was too much work to do and the content of Peter's email was overwhelming her.

She couldn't afford to fail. Again.

"Perhaps another time." With a glance at Ryan,

she lifted her phone. "If you'll excuse us, Ryan and I are having a business meeting."

I don't want to fail. The words drummed in her head.

Cleo glanced at them both and her face coloured as she took her husband's arm. "Sure, we can catch up another time."

They walked away and Jaclyn opened her purse and pulled out her credit card. "What do you want to eat, Ryan? I'll go and order it so we can be quick. I have to get away. I have work to do."

***

Ryan couldn't believe how rude Jaclyn had been to the Kendalls, and he bit back the cross words that sprang to his lips. He stood and pushed his chair back. "No, I'll go and order. I have to use my corporate card. What do you want?"

"Thai Salad, please. The entrée size." Jaclyn stared over his shoulder and didn't meet his eye. Her behaviour was going to go down like a lead balloon in town unless she learned to be a bit more accommodating.

He nodded tersely and made his way to the counter. Cleo and Jon had left the room, probably feeling embarrassed. He placed the order for two salads and raised his voice a little as a surge of noise pushed in from the main bar. "Is there any chance we can have our meals sent quickly. We're in a bit of a hurry."

Well, Jaclyn was.

"Certainly, I'll get them to the kitchen now," the waitress on the till said.

By the time he returned to the table, Jaclyn had her phone on the table and was making notes in a small notepad. She looked up at him, and her face was set. "So what's the bottom line, Ryan? What do you think is the difference in the costing between rebuilding and restoration? Are you happy with the figures that I've been emailed?" She sat back and folded her hands in her lap. "And I want you to be totally honest. I *need* you to be honest with me."

This time Ryan couldn't hold back his reaction; he should have listened to his instincts when he saw Jaclyn in the office yesterday. Instead of bringing her to the pub tonight and thinking they could have a polite and civil meeting, he should have insisted on coming back on Monday and meeting in her office.

She stared at him and his words were low and angry.

"I thought if there was one thing you may have known about me in the time we were seeing each other, is that I have standards. Any figures that I give you will be accurate, and you have no reason to think otherwise."

"Very well. Give me the figures," she said.

"What's the bottom line?"

"The bottom line? The bottom line is that there is a lot more than 'figures' to be considered." He looked at her intently and tried to get through that wall that seemed to be there all the time now. "Jac? What is it with you these days? You know what I'm talking about. You say you want to bring this school forward; There's a lot more than 'cost' involved as you've told me many times yourself. And this community is different to what you're used to. Very different. From what I've heard since I came to town, they've done it tough. But you know what? They pull together. You show this community that you're here to help and make it a great school and they will be behind you every step of the way."

She held his gaze and nodded. "I—" but her words were interrupted by the ringing of her phone. "Excuse me." She pulled out her phone, glanced down and frowned. "I'm sorry I'm going to have to take this." Her chair scraped on the timber floor as she pushed it back and stood. As she walked across the room, and down to the lawn, Ryan was torn. As she spoke into the phone her body language showed defeat. She waved her hand a couple of times, but her back was to him, and he couldn't see her face.

Jaclyn had changed—or maybe he hadn't ever seen her true personality. Now she seemed to be such a loner, but there was a hard side to her that hadn't been obvious before.

He'd been falling in love with her a little bit as they'd gotten to know each other over the three months that they'd been seeing each other and when he had decided to pull back it had hurt.

Jaclyn had been quiet and had withdrawn from him. Maybe it had been wrong not to tell her. He'd known he was moving and hadn't told her.

Then she had been busy every time he'd called, and they had just . . . stopped. There'd never been closure. Ryan stared out over the river waiting for her to come back inside and couldn't help the dull ache that settled around his heart.

Chapter 9

"Dad? What's wrong?" Jaclyn was barely aware of her surroundings as she walked past the beer garden heading for the lawn.

"Where are you, Jaclyn?" Her father's voice held anger and her stomach clenched.

"I'm out for dinner."

"Don't play games with me. You know perfectly well what I mean. *Where* are you? I called Sanctuary Grove today and they said that you've left, and no one seems to know where you are."

"That's not true."

"What? That you've left? Don't lie to me."

She sighed. Her relationship with her father had never been easy and had declined even more when she'd been at university. There was nothing pleasant about their relationship, and there never had been. It would have suited her if Dad didn't contact her at all. One of the positives about being six hours from Sydney; it put distance between them.

"Yes, I have left, but—"

"Can you never stick to anything? Do you know how bad that looks to my colleagues? I was bragging about you being principal of one of the top selective schools in the state."

Not "I'm proud of you". Yes, whatever made her father look good. Nothing ever changed. Jaclyn knew that her strong work ethic was due in part by trying to live up to her father's expectations. Mum had tempered it when she had been alive, and Gran—well, Gran loathed him.

"The only good thing about my Stephanie marrying that selfish man, was you being born," Gran had told her often.

Jaclyn put one hand on her waist and tried to breathe evenly as her stomach clenched again. The river flowed past slowly, and a couple of ducks were paddling along near where she stood. The grass at the edge was green and inviting and she thought how nice it would be simply to walk along the river with no care and no worry. And have no angry father at the other end of the phone.

Serenity? It had been a long time since she'd experienced that.

Jaclyn summoned up all the strength she could find. If Dad ever found out what had happened . . . closing her eyes and taking a deep breath, she steeled herself to be hard.

"Were you calling for a reason, Dad? Other than criticising me? If not, I am in a business meeting. My colleague is waiting for me"

"That's something, I suppose. What colleague? Where are you?"

"Was there anything specific you wanted?"

An angry humph from the other end of the call. "Your grandmother's nursing home has been trying to call you."

"What's wrong? Is Gran okay?"

"I didn't ask. I said I would pass the message on."

"Thank you." *Not.* Jaclyn pressed the disconnect button and looked at the time.

It was heading for seven o'clock, but that meant it was almost nine in New Zealand. She bit her lip wondering if it was too late to call the nursing home. They hadn't ever called her before, so it must be urgent. She stood there tapping her hand on the side of her thigh, and then turned back to the building.

Ryan was waiting patiently, and a bowl of salad was on the table in front of her chair. His expression was hard to read but his voice held concern. "Is everything all right?"

Jaclyn bit her lip again and shrugged. "It was my father, and I'm not sure. I'm sorry, Ryan I'm going to have to cut our meeting short and go and make a call."

She reached down for her bag, and he jumped to his feet.

"Just wait a few seconds." She frowned as he hurried to the counter.

Within a minute he was back with a large takeaway container. He reached over and carefully scooped the salad in, and then snapped the lid shut before handing it to her.

"Here, at least you can take dinner with you. You have to eat."

She took the container and nodded. "Thank you."

"I hope everything is okay with your family. I'll catch up with you next week. There's no urgency."

"That would be good."

"And Jac? Don't let things get to you. I know being out here is a change for you. I'm sorry for speaking hard like I did before."

The kindness in Ryan's voice eased Jaclyn's tension a fraction.

"It's okay. I know you have a good heart, Ryan. Thank you."

Jaclyn turned away and hurried out to the car. She sat there for a moment and steeled herself. There was phone service, and she scrolled through the contacts until she found the number for the Beeches Rest Home in Alexandra.

***

Ryan's meal sat in front of him and he picked at it. The salad was actually tasty, but his appetite had disappeared. The distress on Jaclyn's face had been obvious when she'd come back from her phone call.

He put his fork down and picked up the glass of Coke and drained it. He sat there worrying about Jaclyn, and to a lesser extent, worrying about his reaction to her. His words had been hard, but they'd had to be said. If she was to survive out here at Bindarra Creek—and be happy—she was going to have to shed her city attitude.

She'd lost weight since he'd last seen her. Her face had always been fine, small features with pretty green eyes that tilted up at the corners. In Sydney she had always been made up, and then when they'd had their weekends away, she'd changed. No makeup and comfortable jeans and T-shirts. It was as though she turned into a different person when she was away from the city. Maybe Bindarra Creek would see that change come back.

They'd had some great times together; her demeanour had been happy and she'd always been laughing. He grinned as he thought back to the weekend at Pokolbin in the Hunter Valley. She had a wicked sense of humour and had played a practical joke on him, hiding his keys, because she didn't want to go back to the city.

"Come on Jac, tell me where they are? We're going to hit the peak hour on the M1."

"You find them. They're in something you love." Her eyes had sparkled when he'd grabbed her. "So you're holding them?"

That's the closest he'd ever got to the "L" word.

It had taken him an hour of searching to find them in the freezer of the small fridge in the hotel room, with the ice creams they'd put in there the night before. He closed his eyes and he could still see Jaclyn bending over, holding her sides as laughter overtook her.

That had been the night they'd got back to the city very late, and not because of the traffic, but because they'd ended up back in bed.

Ryan put his hand over his eyes.

What had happened to that Jaclyn?

Had she decided that he was not the right person for her? That he wasn't good enough for her?

She'd seemed fine when they'd driven back to the city that night and had been full of chatter about her promotion and how she was looking forward to leading Sanctuary Gardens High School.

But it was the next week she had started avoiding him.

And now it was as though she was a totally different person.

Ryan shrugged as he pushed his glass away and dug in his pocket for his keys. They were going to have to work together, so he had to sort out his head—and his heart.

He was worried about her, and to see her so

unhappy and tense broke his heart.

As he walked to his ute, he knew he was going to have to try to get to the bottom of what had changed her. He opened the door and as he went to climb in, he remembered that he hadn't filled the tank up today as he'd planned to.

Damn, it was after seven. He turned on his heel and went back into the pub. Jon and Cleo were sitting at the front bar with a plate of hot chips and gravy between them.

"Another drink?" Jon asked.

"No, thanks. I'm heading home now. Where's the best place to get fuel this time of night?"

"If you're quick, Fred's Garage closes at seven thirty."

"Thanks, mate, I'll catch you for a drink one weekend."

"Is Jaclyn all right?" Cleo asked kindly, her dark brown eyes full of concern. "I saw her leave and she looked upset."

Ryan nodded. "Just a problem she had to sort. I'm sorry she was a bit short with you. She's got a lot on her mind. She's a lovely person. Give her a chance."

"Of course. Maybe we can go out for lunch one weekend?"

"Maybe." Ryan turned for the door. "Sorry guys, I have to rush, or you might see me hitchhiking on your way home."

Jon chuckled. "Plenty of room on the back of our ute. But you'd have to share with the dogs."

Ryan laughed as he walked away with a wave. "All good. I'll head to the garage now."

The streets were quiet as he headed through town, and he reached the garage just in time. As he pulled up at the diesel pump an older guy with a shaved head was pulling down the roller door to the workshop.

"Just caught me, mate," he said.

"I'll just fill up." Ryan reached for the nozzle, but the guy walked over and waved him away. "I'll do it. Old-fashioned service here. None of that do it yourself stuff. Fill 'er up, you said?"

"Yes, please." As Ryan waited, a bright blue ute with gleaming paintwork swung into the garage with a deep throaty roar. The driver pulled up at the opposite side of the bowser and climbed out. He touched the brim of his Akubra and nodded at Ryan.

"G'day."

Ryan stepped across to the blue ute from his own dusty white vehicle. "Nice rig."

"Yep, my pride and joy." The guy whipped his Akubra off and tossed it through the open driver's side window. He walked over to Ryan and held out his hand. "You're the bloke who's bought Rossiter's Run, aren't you?"

Ryan nodded and shook the hand offered. "I am. Ryan Rossiter."

The guy's eyes widened. "Wow! You're one of the original Rossiters? Sorry, I'm Daniel. Daniel Stone."

"Good to meet you, Daniel." Ryan shook his head. "Nope, I'm from Werris Creek. The name's a happy coincidence as far as I know."

"Welcome to Bindarra Creek. Jon Kendall told me you'd moved to town. Farming full time out there? It's a good bit of land."

"No such luck. I'm a building inspector with the Department of Education. I work out of Tamworth office, but it's worked out well so far. I'm doing a fair bit of work at the school here."

Daniel nodded. "Ah, since the fire."

"Yep. But I look after the whole region—about forty schools—so I'm only a part-time farmer. One day," Ryan added hopefully.

"Yeah, when this bastard of a drought's over. A lot of us are working a job as well as our properties."

"That'll be sixty-five bucks, thanks." Fred— Ryan assumed that was his name— put the nozzle back into the bowser. "What are you after, Daniel? Didn't I already fill that guzzler of yours up this afternoon?" His laugh was dry and crackly.

As Ryan handed over the cash, Daniel lifted a

container off the back of the ute. "Dad's after some oil for the postie bike, thanks, Fred." He glanced across at Ryan. "You might have met my olds. They run the post office."

"Yeah, I called in to get a post office box a couple of weeks ago. Rob and Lyn?"

"That's them. I suppose Dad wanted to know all about you?"

"No, they were busy the day I was in there. I was surprised to see it so busy. The rest of town was quiet."

"They run a good store, and Dad loves a yarn. Anyway, Ryan, I'll probably see you around. I'll shout you a welcome beer one afternoon."

"Sounds like a plan."

Ryan drove out and headed into the night to make his way home, worry about Jaclyn still settling in him like a rock.

Chapter 10

The front door of Fig Tree Lodge creaked as Jaclyn pushed it open, and she grimaced when she saw a light on in the library. All she wanted to do was have a soak in that inviting deep claw-footed bath that was in the ensuite of her room. She crept up the hall juggling her briefcase and laptop in one hand, and the takeaway salad from the hotel in the other.

She had just walked past the library door when Edwina appeared in the doorway. "Hello, Jaclyn."

Weariness flooded through Jaclyn, but she smiled and fought back a yawn. "Hello."

Edwina raised her eyebrows. "You look tired. A big day?"

Jaclyn shook her head. "A normal day. You know . . . a new school, and lots to learn."

"I heard you had a visit from the paramedics and the fire chief and the police today." Edwina chuckled. "Sounds like you've met half of the town already."

Jaclyn put her briefcase and laptop case on the floor and nodded. "Yes, probably. It's been an interesting day."

Abby Taylor, the senior constable from the police station had been waiting to see her in the foyer when Jaclyn had gone back to her office after waiting for Lea to clear those waiting in her office. The ensuing meeting with Terry Parch's father would have been difficult without the senior constable's presence. In the end, it was decided that it was a police matter and that Abby would interview Terry. Jaclyn was relieved; that was one less thing that she had to deal with, on her first day at Bindarra Creek Central School, but she did process a three-day suspension, dependent on another interview with Terry and his father next week.

After Mr Parch had left, Abby had looked at her sympathetically. "You've had a tough first day. I guess you don't know anyone yet. If you'd like a coffee one day, give me a call."

"Thank you, Abby" Jaclyn had said, "I think I might take you up on that."

Abby leaned back in her chair. "I know what it was like when I transferred here from Dubbo. At first, it's lonely and you feel as though you'll never fit in, but almost overnight you become a part of the community and it feels as though you've been here forever."

Jaclyn laughed. "Can I let you into a secret?"

Abby's green eyes widened with interest and

she nodded.

"I already feel as though I've been here forever and it's actually just over twenty-four hours."

"I hear you're staying at the Fig Tree Inn?"

"Yes. I'll be looking for a place of my own once I learn more about the town."

"You sound like you're planning to be here for a while?"

"At least three years." Jaclyn shrugged. "And who knows. I might decide I like living in the country and stay longer."

"Let's make a coffee date. I know what it's like when you're at work all day. Time gets away. I'm not rostered on Sunday. How about brunch?"

Jaclyn nodded slowly. "If it suits you?"

"It does. My husband, Roman, cooks the boys' breakfast on Sundays and believe me, it would be good to get away until they clean up the mess!"

"How old are your boys?"

"Eddie is in year six and Drew is in the high school. I hope you don't have to ever see Drew in your official capacity." Abby's laugh had been light, but there had been something behind it. "The boys have done it tough over the past couple of years. Roman and I are their foster parents, but they've settled in amazingly well."

"Thanks for the heads-up, Abby. I haven't even had a chance to talk to the staff yet about the students. It's been a hectic beginning."

"Don't let today disillusion you." Abby smiled. "It's a great town, and the school is excellent. *Most* of the staff are dedicated teachers, and without saying anything negative about past leaders, I know they'll appreciate good leadership. I hope you find the school—and the town— to your liking."

Now, Edwina was looking at her with her head tipped to one side. "Would you like to share a cup of chamomile tea with me?" She gestured to the pot on the table next to her chair. "It's very good for reducing stress and helping you sleep."

Jaclyn shook her head. "It's very kind of you, but I have some calls to make before it's too late."

A little white lie because she'd already rung the aged care facility, but she just wanted to lock herself in her room and go to bed.

"I hope you sleep well. Would you like breakfast in the morning?"

"No, thank you. Seeing it's Saturday, I might go for an explore in the town."

Edwina nodded as Jaclyn picked up her briefcase and laptop. "A good plan. There should be a few people out and about. It's going to be a clear and warm day."

"That sounds good."

"Good night. I hope you sleep well," she said again.

Jaclyn climbed the stairs and opened the door to her room with an audible sigh of relief. Placing the salad on the small table next to the kettle, and a cup and saucer, she headed for the bathroom, and turned the taps onto full. She stood there for a moment and wondered if she should be conserving water. Edwina had said nothing about the drought, and there were no signs in the bathroom.

A range of bath products lined the shelf beneath the window and Jaclyn picked up a small bottle of lavender bath gel and held it beneath the hot water. The soothing fragrance surrounded her, and she inhaled as it mingled with the steam drifting up from the hot water.

Erring on the side of water conservation, she turned the taps off when there was a reasonable amount of water in the tub. She went into the bedroom and pulled out her bathrobe. Stripping off, she eased herself into the deliciously hot water.

Such a shame. If she was in the city in her apartment, it would be neck deep. She would have to get used to this country life.

At least the call to New Zealand had eased her worry.

Gran had been taken to hospital as a precaution yesterday, but it had turned out to be a heavy chest cold. She was on the mend now and had returned to the home this morning. The woman on reception had taken the phone into her grandmother's room so Jaclyn could be reassured.

"I'm fine, Jaclyn. Don't you worry about me. There's a lot of life left in this old bird yet." Her Scottish accent had brought a smile to Jaclyn's face "How did you know I was ill anyway?"

"Dad rang."

A snort came through the phone. "Pfft."

"I'm going to come and visit you soon. There's a long weekend coming up; I'm going to look at flights later."

"Don't be silly, lass. I told you, I'm fine."

Jaclyn had rested her head against the car window. "I know but I still want to come and see you." Her voice trembled. "I need a Gran hug."

"In that case you'd better get yourself over here. But really is it worth it for a weekend, sweetheart?"

"Of course, it is. It's only a three-hour flight to Queenstown." Jaclyn wasn't going to mention the six-hour plus drive each way to and from Sydney to get to the airport. That piece of news was for a face-to-face visit, not for delivering over the phone.

"Let me know when you're coming, Jaclyn. I'd better go now, the dragon from the desk is giving me a dirty look."

"I will." Jaclyn chuckled. She knew how much the staff loved Gran. She was a beautiful woman, inside and out. "Love you, Gran."

"And I love you too. You take care of yourself."

Now she rested her head against the back of the bath tub and let the lavender and hot water do its work.

Maybe not the serenity she'd craved, but a lightness that hadn't been there earlier.

***

Jaclyn was surprised to see it was after nine o'clock when she reached for her phone and checked the time the next morning. She'd been tempted to roll over and snuggle into the luxuriously soft feather pillow and go back to sleep until she'd seen how late it was.

She climbed out of bed and stretched before crossing to the window and lifting the lace curtain. It was sunny and clear as Edwina had forecast. And it was amazing what sunny skies and a good night's sleep did for your disposition. As she spotted the untouched salad on the table, her stomach grumbled. After her bath last night Jaclyn had fallen into bed—no work had been touched—and she had slept deeply and dreamlessly.

Looking at the salad brought Ryan to mind. She had been rude to him—and other people—over the past few days, and guilt rippled through her. It was not the way to deal with her situation. Okay, so things had gone wrong for her and it was out of her control, but there was no need to take it out on others who had nothing to do with the situation. It was a new day—a beautiful day—and she would treat it as a new start. The school here had its challenges, but she was in the leadership role and she would lead. She stood at the window looking into the branches of the beautiful tree as a pretty bird flitted in and out of the branches.

I'm here for three years, and I'll make the most of it. It was a vow she would focus on and a vow she would keep.

Small steps and one at a time.

After a quick wash in the bathroom, Jaclyn pulled out a pair of white Capri pants and a pink T-shirt. On the way back from New Zealand in a couple of weeks, she'd call into her apartment and collect the rest of her clothes; she hadn't been thinking clearly when she'd packed for the drive to Bindarra Creek. She was happy to let the apartment sit empty.

This morning she'd explore the town, and this afternoon she'd make use of the small alcove in her room, set up her laptop and get some work done. Tomorrow, she'd have brunch with Abby, and the weekend would be over before she knew it. She would make Monday her first successful day at Bindarra Creek Central School.

There was no sign of life in the lodge as she made her way downstairs. Closing the door behind her and stepping out onto the front path, she looked up for the pretty bird, but it had disappeared. Taking a deep breath, Jaclyn set off on her exploration, heading for the main street of town. Coffee was her first goal for the day and then she would see what panned out. Her car was parked outside, and she frowned, wondering how safe it was to leave it out on the street. She had to get to know the town, and she was hoping that Abby would be able to fill her in tomorrow.

Turning right at the gate, it was only a short walk to the corner, and she looked across the road to the café where she had smelled the delectable coffee aroma the other day.

The Cyprus Café had Greek-style columns at the front. A young woman with glossy black hair was standing at an outside table chatting to a couple of women. Heat ran up into her face as she realised it was Cleo, the woman from the pub last night.

Right, small steps, but an essential one.

Jaclyn crossed the road and waited for the waitress to leave the table. The pretty girl gave her a wide smile as she walked back into the café and Jaclyn returned it with a friendly nod and smile.

"Morning, Cleo," she said brightly moving closer to the table.

"Oh, hello, Jaclyn," Cleo smiled, but Jaclyn sensed it was forced.

"I owe you an apology for last night. I was tired, but that's no excuse for being rude. I'm sorry."

"That's fine. Don't give it another thought, we all have bad days." Cleo pointed to the empty seat beside the older woman. "Would you like to join us? Jaclyn, this is my grandmother, Esther Ainslie. Gran, this is Jaclyn, the new principal at the high school. She was having a meeting with Ryan Rossiter last night when we were at the pub."

Jaclyn hesitated and clutched her purse wondering if she should accept. Maybe Cleo was just being polite? "Thank you. I'd love to join you, if you're sure? I don't want to intrude."

"Of course, we are," Esther said. "Edwina told me you were staying at Fig Tree Lodge. Thalia just took our order, so you go in and order what you want, and then we'll have a chat. I'm guessing you don't know many people in Bindarra Creek yet?"

"No, I don't. I only arrived on Thursday. I did know Ryan in Sydney." Jaclyn smiled shyly as her cheeks heated again. There was no need to say any more about how well she had known Ryan a few months ago. "I'll go in and order and be back in a moment. Thank you."

Bunting of Greek and Australian flags hung along freshly-painted blue and white walls, making the red seats in the booths along the far wall stand out and the delectable smell of coffee filled the café.

Jaclyn headed for the till where a blackboard menu was displayed on the right-hand wall. A delectable display of cakes and pastries that would rival any upmarket Sydney *patisserie* filled the glass-fronted display cabinets. As she stood there reading the menu a woman came through the door that Jaclyn assumed led to the kitchen.

"Thalia, your papa would like you to restock the coffee shelves," she said with a glance at Jaclyn. "I'll take over the till."

The pretty young woman—Thalia—winked at Jaclyn as she came past her carrying a small cardboard box. "Yes, Mama."

Jaclyn browsed the menu and then looked at the display shelves. "Oh, it all looks so beautiful. She pointed to a frittata-looking dish in the heated cabinet. "What's that?"

"You have good taste. My husband, Stavros, made that fresh this morning. We will have many customers for brunch over the weekend and it is a favourite with the locals. It is a Greek sausage casserole, with feta cheese and artichoke hearts." Her smile was wide.

"Yum. I'll have one serve of that please, with a double shot espresso. I'm sitting with the ladies outside."

As the woman rang up the sale, she looked curiously at Jaclyn. "You are friend or family with the Ainslies?"

Jaclyn smiled. "I am Jaclyn Douglas. I've just moved to town."

"Ah the new high school principal. Welcome, welcome." She turned to the kitchen. "Stavros, come out of the kitchen. Thalia, come and be introduced."

As Jaclyn pulled her purse out of her small shoulder bag, the woman waved her hand. "No, no money today. It is our welcome to you." Her smile was wide. "We are Thea and Stavros Levonis, and this is our daughter, Thalitsa."

"Thalia," the young woman said as she walked back around behind the counter. "I hope we see you in our café again."

"I'm sure you will. The coffee smells divine."

"We are here to please," Stavros said.

The day was already going well, and she hadn't even had her first coffee. Jaclyn slipped her purse into her bag and headed back to the table outside.

"So did you get the third degree from the lovely Thea?" Esther asked.

"No, just a lovely welcome and a complimentary breakfast." Jaclyn looked around. "I'm beginning to like Bindarra Creek already."

"That's excellent. Where are you going to live? Do you have a family coming to join you?"

Jaclyn shook her head. "No, it's just me."

Cleo cleared her throat. "Do you mind if I ask you something?"

Uh oh. Jaclyn hated that. It always meant something personal was going to be asked. Before she could answer, Thalia came out with a tray of coffee and pastries.

"Here you are ladies. Jaclyn, your breakfast is on the way."

"Thank you."

Thalia went back inside, and Jaclyn turned to Cleo. "What did you want to ask me?"

"Um, I just wonder if you came out here because Ryan was here. I sort of got the impression that you were a couple last night. I saw the way he looked at you when you went outside."

Jaclyn knew her fair cheeks would be glowing red and she tried to keep her voice normal.

"No," she replied with a quiet chuckle. "Neither of us knew the other was out here until we met at the school when I arrived on Thursday. We were both as surprised as each other."

Cleo nodded slowly, and Jaclyn took the opportunity to pick up her coffee.

Esther threw a disapproving glance at Cleo. "Please excuse my granddaughter's curiosity. Since she and Jon got married last year, she's turned into a regular matchmaker. You want everyone to be as happy as you pair are, don't you, Cleo?"

"Nothing wrong with that." Cleo positively glowed.

"I'm happy for you, Cleo," Jaclyn said, and she meant it. She turned back to Esther. "Now as far as where I'm going to live, I'd like to eventually buy my own place, but until I get to know the town, I'm looking for somewhere to live temporarily."

Esther nodded. "Would you be happy boarding for a while?"

"I would. Especially if there were meals provided. I'm going to be busy over the first few months at the school."

"Would it bother you if you were close to the school?" Esther asked with a frown. "Although we're such a small town, wherever you live the students will soon find out."

Jaclyn shook her head. "It would probably be convenient. Do you know of something?"

"I do. My friend Gemma Haydon—she was a teacher at the school before she retired—lives in Wilgara Avenue next to the sports oval."

"That's beside the school, isn't it? Jaclyn asked.

"It is, and Gemma has a room to rent and meals are included. She's a wonderful cook. I can introduce you if you'd like?"

"That's sounds good to me, thank you. Perhaps tomorrow afternoon?"

"Leave it with me. Ah, Here's your breakfast."

Jaclyn's eyes widened as she looked at the laden plate. "I think I'll need a big walk after this."

##

After she finished the meal and arranged to meet Esther at her friend's house early the following afternoon, Jaclyn took a walk around the town. As much as she hated to admit it, and knew he probably wouldn't be in town anyway, she kept an eye out for Ryan's white ute. Hearing what Cleo had said about the way he'd looked at her last night had made Jaclyn feel good—yet uncomfortable.

As much as she found Ryan Rossiter attractive, she didn't want to start up a relationship again. The way things were, she had to focus on her work at school one hundred percent and ger her career back on track.

Jaclyn wandered around the town and was surprised by how many people said hello or wished her a good morning. She explored the small business centre of town, and then determined to walk off that huge breakfast, she headed the way they had driven last night to the hotel. Walking past the Riverside Hotel she crossed Kingfisher Bridge heading for the park on the other side. It wouldn't hurt to sit for a while, watch the ducks and gather her thoughts as she got herself into work mode for the afternoon. As Jaclyn crossed the bridge towards the park, angry voices reached her. She paused and listened and then the smell of cigarettes drifted up to her with another angry voice.

"If you don't have the money next time, jerk, I won't come back again. You don't get it for nothing, do you hear?"

As she watched a pimply-faced youth ran out from beneath the bridge and headed for a dark green sedan that was parked outside the hotel. He got into the passenger side and when he had slammed the door shut, the car took off with a loud squeal of tyres. It did a U-turn at the first corner and then roared over the bridge heading north.

With a shrug she memorised the number plate and kept walking, but when she reached the other side of the river and turned towards the park, Jaclyn glanced back. A young boy in a black hoodie was leaning against the first pylon on the other side at the edge of the water; she was sure it was the Parch boy who had started the fires at the school yesterday.

And Jaclyn was equally sure she had just witnessed a failed drug deal.

Chapter 11

"I like the look of this town." Joe looked around as Ryan drove past Fig Tree Lodge. He could have taken a more direct route to the SES building on River Road, but they had come to town a bit earlier than they needed to so they could pick up some lunch before the meeting. He was surprised to see Jaclyn's car parked in the street there; he thought she would have been at the school working. Frowning, he turned left into Main Street; he was spending way too much time thinking about Jaclyn.

"What are you looking so pissed off about?"

Ryan shook his head as his brother looked at him quizzically. "I'm not. I was just thinking about where we'd get some lunch. What do you feel like?"

Joe chuckled. "Um . . . KFC?"

"Sorry. You're in the country now. How about some takeaway chicken and chips? I know the café around the corner does that."

Joe nodded and Ryan pulled into a vacant car park across the road from the antiques shop. His heart kicked up a beat or three as Jaclyn walked around the corner. She looked casual and relaxed as she strolled along. He hurried to get out of the ute before she turned down Willow Drive towards Fig Tree Lodge.

"Jaclyn," he called. Ryan was pleased to see her smile when she spotted him, and hurried across the road to where she waited on the corner outside the beauty salon.

"Hi," he said when he reached her. "You look different today."

She looked down and gestured to her clothes. "I didn't think the corporate suit was quite right for Saturday morning exploring Bindarra Creek."

"I meant more relaxed."

"I am. I've been exploring and I had breakfast with Cleo and her grandmother." Her eyes were glowing, and Ryan found it hard to look away.

"And what have you explored?"

"Not a lot. Would you believe I've been sitting over in the park watching the ducks for ages."

Ryan reached over and pretended to take her temperature. " Is this the real Jaclyn Douglas?"

She looked at him with a guilty nod. "I should be working, but I needed to chill."

"Chill is good," he said quietly.

"Jaclyn?" Joe's voice interrupted them. "Is this your Jaclyn from Sydney?"

Before Ryan could answer, Joe stepped past him and held his hand out to her. "Hi, I'm Joe, this galoot's little brother."

Even though Ryan was embarrassed, Jaclyn's laugh warmed his heart.

"Galoot?" she said. "I haven't heard that for years. My grandmother used to say it all the time."

"Thanks, Joe. Love you too, bro."

Joe nudged him with his shoulder. "I'll leave you pair to catch up. I'm going to get some lunch." He whistled as he headed towards the café.

The silence was heavy and then Jaclyn and Ryan both went to speak at the same time.

He shook his head. "You first."

"I was just going to ask you why you were in town today. How far out is your place?"

"About forty ks," he said. "Joe and I have come in to join the SES."

"That's good. You always said you wanted to be a part of a rural community." Their eyes met and held again, and Jaclyn's cheeks coloured. "Well, I'd better let you go. I'm going to go back and do some work for the afternoon."

"Don't work too hard," he said, and then couldn't help himself. "And Jac, it's good to see *you* back."

With a nod, he left her standing there and followed his brother into the café.

***

It took Jaclyn a good hour to focus before she settled into her work. If she looked to the right, she could see the street outside from the small desk in the alcove in the room, and she had to force herself to stop looking outside.

Good to see *me* back? What did Ryan mean by that? Her heart had skittered like a silly teenager's when they'd been standing outside on the footpath. And how did his brother know about them in Sydney? She wondered what Ryan had said for Joe to call her "his Jaclyn from Sydney"?

She chastised herself; she was spending way too much energy thinking about Ryan Rossiter; she needed to focus solely on the work she had to do. She'd found some school policy and procedures documents on the school network, as well as a current staff list and intended learning as much about the school as she could over the weekend. Monday she would be friendly and firm, but professional.

But how good had Ryan looked in that snug fitting black T-shirt? He was tall and broad, and she wouldn't have been surprised to hear that he'd been working out. His shirt had hugged that tightly-muscled chest more than it had a few months ago. Or maybe it was the work he was doing on his farm.

Stop it! Jaclyn swallowed and turned back to the laptop. The list of permanent administrative and teaching staff in the high school filled the screen.

So far, she had met Lea and Kellie and knew

she had work to do with both of them. There was
another part-time admin staff member on the list,
and Jaclyn assumed she'd meet her next week. She
ran her finger down the high school staff. Curlew—
she'd seen him on Thursday. David Kepple: Acting
Deputy and cream-bun lover. She grinned and
rolled her eyes.

Soon, all—well almost all—thoughts of Ryan
had disappeared, and Jaclyn immersed herself in the
policies of Bindarra Creek School. The out-of-date
policies, but it did give her a feel for where she
needed to begin.

A couple of hours later, she stood and stretched,
before picking up the small kettle and filling it with
water. As she waited for it to boil, her laptop dinged
with an incoming email and she walked back to the
small desk. Jaclyn raised her eyebrows, surprised to
see another email from Peter Hughes.

The kettle clicked off, but she ignored it.

*Hi Jaclyn. I hope you've settled into the school.
I knew I could email you on the weekend as I know
we have the same work ethic.*

She frowned. What a strange thing to say. Peter
had only worked with her for five months before
she'd left Sanctuary Gardens, and their management
styles had been very different. He had been a
difficult deputy at times—and she wouldn't have
said that his work ethic was anything to comment

on. He'd spent a lot of time wandering around the school talking to students. Then again, she couldn't judge him on that. Being a principal and dealing with the constant requirements and expectations of a data-driven organisation made it hard to find the time to leave the office. It was something she would focus on at Bindarra Creek, so maybe Peter had had the right idea. She leaned closer to the computer and scrolled down; his email was long.

I hope you have already given a great deal of thought to the building situation at BCC and taken my advice seriously. It is essential that the buildings are demolished, and that the advice given by the regional office is not given credence. However, please don't repeat that. It wouldn't create a harmonious relationship.

I know you will be wanting to fit in with the community, but you need to know that there are those outside of it who want to see you fail. Trust me, Jaclyn. I am on your side.

I admired your work in the short time we worked together at Sanctuary Gardens and I know that you were innocent of any wrongdoing. I know who it was who set you up to take the fall, and they are still determined to see you fail even in a minor school like Bindarra Creek. Eyes are watching from afar, so please be warned.

Jaclyn, I have to come out to the western region

in a couple of weeks and I will be able to tell you more. In the meantime, watch your back and don't trust anyone. His reach is far and wide.

Warm regards

Peter.

Jaclyn put her hand against her churning stomach.

His reach? Whose reach?

For a moment as she'd read those words, she had thought she was going to throw up. *Who on earth was Peter talking about?* She knew she'd been set up at Sanctuary Gardens, but she had no idea why or who was responsible.

It sounded as though Peter had known all along. So why hadn't he told her then? She would have been able to defend herself at that dreadful interview with the director.

Shutting down the laptop. Jaclyn put her head in her hands and closed her eyes. A headache was building behind her temples and her fingers were tingling. She pressed her fingers against the sides of her forehead and focused on her breathing.

She had to get out of the room. Outside into fresh air and away from that email. She didn't what to read it again, trying to figure out who Peter was talking about, until she felt better.

Picking up her purse, Jaclyn pushed open the door and hurried down the stairs and out into the spring afternoon.

A coffee. A strong coffee. And the river. She could watch the ducks again and try to get her thoughts in order. Her heart thudded and her fingers tingled and prickled as she closed the door behind her harder than she should have.

Chapter 12

The SES mob were a fun bunch, and Ryan and Joe were happy to adjourn to the hotel after they'd joined up and were given a short orientation briefing, and an information pack to take home to read.

"Good to have you onboard, guys. Next meeting is three weeks today," Kel Jones said.

Ryan had been pleased to see a few familiar faces at the SES headquarters this afternoon. Fred from the garage had greeted him with a handshake, Abby, the policewoman he'd met at the school was there, and of course, Mandy.

"Do you want a lift to the pub, Joe?" Mandy had latched onto Joe. His younger brother had always been a flirt and Ryan shot him a warning glance.

Joe shrugged and ignored him. "Sure." He looped an arm around Mandy's shoulders, and they walked out together.

Ryan shook his head and walked to his ute and put his information pack on the front seat. Joe was grown up now and Ryan had to accept he wasn't responsible for him these days. Hell, the number of times he'd had to bail him out of trouble at Werris Creek when Joe had been in his teens were too many to remember.

Ryan started the ute and pulled into the street, and before he knew what he was doing he put the indicator on to turn into Church Street, past the cemetery and then left into Willow Drive. As he approached Fig Tree Lodge, a small figure in white pants and a pink T-shirt ran down the path to the gate.

It was Jaclyn and she was bent over, her arms crossed against her chest.

Ryan hit the brakes and pulled up suddenly as she stepped onto the footpath. She looked over at the ute; her eyes were wide, and her cheeks streaked with tears. She looked past him, put her head down and hurried along the street towards Main Street.

Ryan jumped out of the ute and ran after her. "Jac! Wait up!"

She ignored him and kept going. Finally, he caught up to her, and ran past her turning around to face her front on.

"Jaclyn? What's wrong?"

The face that looked back at him was very different to the one that had held laughter only a few short hours ago. She looked at him blindly and her lips trembled as she tried to answer.

"I—" She shook her head and tears welled in her eyes.

Ryan took her arm and spoke gently. "Where

were you going?"

"Coffee. The river." Her breath was coming in short gasps and he thought she was going to hyperventilate. He couldn't help himself; he put his arms around her and held her close. She rested her head on his shoulder.

"I want you to concentrate on breathing in and breathing out slowly. Okay? Can you do that, Jac?"

A brief nod against his T-shirt. Slowly Jaclyn's breathing eased, and Ryan shut his eyes as he held her close. His hands were firm against her back, and he could feel how thin she was. She'd lost a lot of weight since he'd last held her.

Finally, she took in a trembling breath. "Thank you. I'm okay now."

Slowly he let go and she stepped back. Her face was pale with a red spot high on each of her cheekbones.

"How about I walk to the river with you? We'll get a coffee on the way."

"Thank you. That would be nice."

It seemed natural to take her hand in his and Jaclyn didn't pull away as he enfolded her hand in his. Her fingers were ice-cold despite the warmth of the clear October afternoon.

They walked quietly together and crossed the road when they reached the corner.

"The café is closed," Ryan said. "How about we

go and sit on this side of the river at the back of the
beer garden at the pub? I think a brandy might be
the trick for you."

She nodded mutely, and he held her hand firmly
as he led her around the corner, through the pub car
park, and across the lawn to a table at the edge of
the river. Ryan gestured to the seat and she sat
down slowly, and he sat beside her.

"I don't want to leave you to get your drink until
I know you're okay."

"I'm okay now." Jaclyn lifted her face to him,
and her eyes were clear as she returned his gaze
steadily. "Thank you. I was in the middle of a panic
attack when you called me. It's gone now."

"Are you sure?"

She nodded and looked down at their joined
hands. "I'm sure."

"What would you like to drink. They probably
do coffee here if you'd prefer that?"

This time her pale lips tilted in a tentative smile.
"As my gran would say, I think a dram of whisky
would do me a power of good."

"Wait here. Promise to stay?"

Jaclyn nodded again and Ryan let go of her
hand. He hurried across the lawn and took the steps
two at a time. Joe and Mandy were sitting on two
stools at the bar inside.

"Do me a favour, Joe. Drink light beer and drive

us home later?"

Joe shrugged. "I'm easy. If you want. I thought you'd got lost."

Ryan shook his head. "I passed Jaclyn on the way. We're going to sit down the back and have a chat."

"Fair enough. Hope things go the way you'd like them to. She seems nice."

Mandy was following the conversation wide-eyed. Ryan squeezed Joe's shoulder. "Me too, bro."

***

Jaclyn looked up as Ryan approached the table carrying two glasses. Her stomach curled when he smiled at her and lifted the two glasses.

"I hope you don't mind but I got two shots each to save going back to the bar."

"Thank you. I'll sip it slowly."

He sat beside her on the same side of the table facing the river, and his leg was warm against her thigh. The sun was dropping towards the horizon and the western sky was fading to mauve.

Jaclyn lifted her glass and took a sip, and the whisky burned a warm path down her throat and into her stomach. She held up the glass and looked at the amber liquid as it swirled in the glass. "You remembered? Glenfiddich?"

"The only whisky worth drinking, I recall." His

voice was low and husky, and something shifted in her. She moved away a little to break that connection. She wasn't in any state of mind to trust her feelings—no matter how pleasant they were.

"Gran and I went to the distillery when she took me to Scotland for my twenty-first birthday." Jaclyn gestured to the river and the ducks that were still paddling along with the current. "I was thinking about that day when I sat here this morning. There's a small lake at the front of the building and the day we were there they were paddling around and every so often they would all dive like synchronised swimmers." She couldn't help the giggle that came with the memory and felt Ryan relax next to her. "We were doubled up with laughter watching their little bums waggle in sequence, and when the rest of the tour group looked at us as though we were mad, we laughed even harder. Gran had tears running down her cheeks and I can still hear her saying "*yer* bums are *oot* the water, duckies.""

"Can I assume this was after the whisky tasting?" Ryan's eyes crinkled as she looked up at him.

Jaclyn nodded. "You can."

He pointed to the river. "Well I hope our Aussie ducks have more manners than their Sottish counterparts."

"I'm sure they do." She looked down and held

her glass with both hands.

His voice was quiet as he moved his head closer to hers, and he was so close, his breath fanned her cheek.

"Jac?"

She looked up into blue eyes that were very close to hers. "Yes, Ryan?"

"You're not sick, arc you, Jac? You've lost a lot of weight in the last six months."

She shook her head. "No, but I haven't been eating much. I've had a bit of stress to deal with."

"Want to talk about it?"

She bit her lip. "I was about to tell you the other day when Dave interrupted us. And then I thought better of it. I was awful to you, Ryan. It was in the middle of it all happening and I couldn't help myself. I didn't know who to talk to. I didn't know where to turn and I couldn't believe what happened to me." She put her head down again and watched as his hand took hers again. "I didn't know who I could tell, and I knew what high standards you have, so I couldn't risk it."

"Do you want to start at the beginning?" His voice was soft as his thumb caressed the back of her hand.

Jaclyn swallowed and took a deep breath, determined not to go into panic mode again. She'd had too many of those attacks in the past few months and hated losing control.

"Take it slow. Start when you're ready."

"I trust you Ryan, and I want you to know that everything I tell you is the absolute truth. No one has believed me yet. That's why I didn't know where to turn. Every time someone listened to my story, I sounded guilty and as though I was making excuses, but I *didn't* do anything wrong." Her breath hitched and Ryan dropped her hand and put his arm around her shoulders.

She closed her eyes and took in his warmth, and the comfort of his hold.

"Would it make it easier if I told you how much I've missed you, Jac? What a gap it left in my life when we . . . when I guess . . . when we just stopped. We didn't even break up, did we?"

She shook her head. "No." A fierce surge of strength flooded through her as Ryan's lips brushed her forehead and Jaclyn knew she could finally tell her story and be listened to and believed without any fear of being judged.

Chapter 13

Jaclyn's voice was low, and Ryan moved closer to hear her soft words and to block the sounds drifting across from the pub.

"I'd only been at Sanctuary Gardens for five months and the school was humming along like clockwork. The students were engaged, and the majority of the staff were onboard with the new initiatives that I'd introduced." She paused and took a deep breath. "There were a couple of older and longer serving male staff members who didn't like having a female boss, but I could cope with that. I'd interviewed a couple of them about some breaches of policy, and one who took sick leave every Wednesday."

"Every Wednesday?" Ryan interrupted sensing Jaclyn needed a flow in the spill of words that were tumbling from her lips faster with each sentence.

"Yes, I knew he was going surfing. His head teacher had told me how he bragged in the staffroom about missing sports duty every Wednesday and the double period with his difficult year eight class. The rest of the staffroom were pretty upset with him, so when his supervisor told me what he was doing, and after I'd received a letter from the department telling *me* to request a medical certificate from him for each sick day, I called him in for a chat."

"And?"

"He admitted it, and he cried, and said he wasn't coping with teaching and that he needed a mental health day each week. I was kind and sympathetic and told him about the employee counselling service. Foolishly, it was just the two of us in the office when I spoke to him." She shook her head. "Boy, did I learn a lesson there."

"When State Office rang the next week to say that the director wanted an appointment with me, at first I was pretty excited, and then in the next sentence his personal assistant suggested *I* might like to have a support person at the meeting. I was still feeling pretty arrogant and I didn't understand why I would need one."

Ryan shook his head. "I think I know where this is going."

Jaclyn touched his arm. "No, it went much further than that. Yes, I was charged with bullying a staff member, because he made up a huge story about how I'd ripped into him and threatened him with dismissal in that interview. It was his word against mine."

"They didn't trust your professional word?

Disgraceful."

"It wasn't only that. That was only a minor part of the investigation. The main reason that the director wanted to see me was about the school finances. They had sent the auditors in the week before when I was at a conference to investigate some discrepancies in the accounts."

Ryan took her hand. He could see where this was heading. "Did he ask you to explain it?"

Jaclyn shook her head. "I was never given the chance. I wasn't even told what account the missing money had come from. Apparently, I had signed six cheques to the value of thirty thousand dollars over a period of three weeks. Cheques that went to a bogus company and were banked, and then of course, the company was untraceable. They were payments for some repair work and new carpeting in the older buildings. I'd hired the contractors and seen the work completed so I had no reason to doubt the payments or the codes the money came from."

"So you were found guilty of financial fraud? Were the police called in?"

"No." This time her head shake was swift. "I demanded that they be contacted, but the director said that it wasn't significant enough, which was a load of—"

"Bullshit." Ryan's words were terse as he

squeezed her fingers.

"Yes. I wasn't found guilty of anything *officially*, but the director told me I was not a fit person to be running the school if that had happened, and that I was ultimately responsible as I'd signed the cheques."

"How?"

"It's the way the system works in all public schools. The cheques come in from the bursar, who has received the invoice and cross checks it against an original order. The print out comes to the principal who decides which code the payment comes from or requests the information from the person in charge of that particular program. The bursar does the final check of amounts and codes and then the cheques are written, a report is printed out with the order and the invoice. The principal signs the two documents and the cheque, and then they go to the deputy for the second signature."

"It sounds like a secure system."

"It is, and I can't understand what happened. My financial officer in the school was excellent."

"Did he—she— take the fall with you?"

"No, she didn't, because I was the principal and, I was held responsible for any error in the system."

Jaclyn stared ahead at the river, and any mirth about the Scottish ducks was long gone. "I was given the option of taking a demotion to deputy principal in the city, or failing that of going to state office while the matter was investigated further."

"And what did you choose?"

"I refused demotion and went to the head office expecting a fair hearing and that justice would prevail." Her laugh was bitter. "I certainly grew up fast. I spent two weeks photocopying and there was no further investigation. It was all swept under the carpet." She sat back and took her hand from his. "Then Bindarra Creek came up and I was offered that. And here I am."

***

Ryan walked Jaclyn home before Joe drove them back to the farm. He stood at the gate of Fig Tree Lodge with her and as she looked up into his face, the evening darkness shadowed his features. His eyes were intense, but his mouth was tight.

For the first time in weeks, Jaclyn felt as though a burden had been lifted. Ryan had believed her, and it was a good feeling.

He'd insisted on buying them hamburgers and chips for dinner and they'd sat at the back table as the night came in; the sounds from the pub above them quietened as people drifted home. Around seven o'clock the soft conversation coming from the pub was overlaid by country and western music, but to her relief it was kept at a low volume.

"Just as well my landlady's not here," Jaclyn

152

said with a smile after she wiped the barbeque sauce from her lips. "She hates country music. You'll have to meet Edwina, she's a character."

Jaclyn had devoured the hamburger and enjoyed it, as she had her Greek casserole breakfast this morning. At this rate she would have to exercise twice a day.

"Yes, I heard the girls at the SES talking about her this afternoon. Apparently, they were all going to have a psychic reading tonight."

"Oh," Jaclyn said thoughtfully. "I can see her doing that. Maybe I should get her opinion on whether it's worth sticking it out here at Bindarra, or just walking away from my career."

Ryan held her arms firmly. "Don't even think about it. That would be giving whoever set you up a win. You're going to do a great job and show them up in Sydney. Then you can go back there to a big school when you've done your work here."

Jaclyn stood on her tiptoes and brushed a kiss across Ryan's cheek. He needed a shave and the rasp of his whiskers was pleasant. "Thank you for believing me. You don't know what a boost it's given me. Monday is a new day, and I'm going to have a good week.

"I'm pleased to hear that."

And I'm going to keep my wits about me and watch out for anything strange. She had said nothing to Ryan about Peter's email, and that made her feel a little guilty. Was it because Ryan was part of the regional properties department that Peter was whistleblowing on, or was it because she was honouring the confidentiality of a colleague's email?

Jaclyn wasn't sure, but she was going to be very careful.

"So you're okay now? If I go home?"

She nodded. "I am, thank you. No more silly panic attacks. I've put them behind me now.

"What brought it on this afternoon?" Jaclyn's face heated and she was pleased it was dark. She waved her hand vaguely. "Oh, just thinking about it, I guess. New surroundings and the unknown week ahead."

"I've got trips out into the region early next week. Would you like me to come in and check on you tomorrow?"

It would have been nice to spend more time in Ryan's company, but Jaclyn shook her head. "No. I'm fine. You've got work to do and I'm having brunch with Abby, and then Esther is taking me to meet a potential new landlady. Room and board."

Ryan nodded. "A busy day. And if I'd had more time to get the farmhouse shipshape you would have been welcome to stay out there."

"Thank you, but I'm a big girl now. I can look

after myself."

"Can you, Jac?" Before she could move, Ryan's arms went around her back and he pulled her close. His deep blue eyes held her gaze and warmth crept through Jaclyn as he lowered his head and his lips gently took hers.

It was a gentle kiss full of promise and when he lifted his head, she reached up and touched his rough cheek.

"Goodnight, Ryan, and thank you," she whispered.

"Goodnight. Sweet dreams."

She stood at the gate and watched until he disappeared around the corner.

##

Jaclyn slept well and the heaviness that had dogged her for the past few weeks had eased considerably when she woke up early on Sunday morning. A small smile played about her lips as she relived Ryan's kiss. How could it be that less than one day ago, unhappiness and frustration had dogged her, and now on the next day, hope unfurled within her. Hope that her new job in this small town was going to work out. How could one person make her feel so different in such a short time?

The answer was because of how she felt about that one person. She had been falling in love with Ryan Rossiter six months ago, but she had moved away from him and focused on her new job. Jaclyn knew she had withdrawn into herself and convinced herself that she didn't need anybody.

Ryan's actions and care and concern for her wellbeing had brought her to life last night and eased that worry.

Today was a bright new day and she was going to make the most of it. She jumped out of bed and headed for the shower. It would be a few days until she saw Ryan again, and it would give her a chance to put her thoughts—and feelings— into perspective.

Abby had agreed to meet her at the Cyprus Café at nine, but Jaclyn headed there early. She was content to sit there with a coffee, read the papers and watch the world go by as she waited.

Right on nine a police paddy wagon pulled up across the road, and Jaclyn was surprised to see Abby climb out, dressed in uniform. The policewoman sat on the chair opposite her and sighed.

"So much for my Sunday. Roman and I were going to take the boys kayaking when I got home, but I got called in. AJ's got the flu apparently, so I drew the short straw." Abby grinned. "My three men weren't impressed. I told them seeing I had to work, they did too, and I drew up a list of chores."

Thalia came out to the table with her pencil

poised. "Morning, ladies. I heard you say you got called in, Abby? So did I. Mama decided she had something important to do at home, so being the dutiful daughter, I had to come in too." Thalia gestured dramatically to the sky. "And look at this gorgeous spring day. Kel was going to take me for a drive down to Tamworth to the shops, but it'll be too late when I finish here.

Jaclyn smiled. "You two are making me feel guilty not having to go to work today."

"Don't feel guilty, Jaclyn. I'm sure you're going to have a few busy weeks ahead while you settle in." Thalia took their orders and went back inside.

"Speaking of keeping busy, did you know there's a P&C meeting this Wednesday night at the school?" Abby leaned back in her chair.

"No, I guess I'll catch up on everything tomorrow. Friday was a bit of a write off at school."

"It's also going to be a bit of a welcome function for you, and there's already a lot of interest. You'll meet a lot of people there."

"Oh. Okay." Even though she was feeling good, Jaclyn didn't know if she was ready for that yet. She wanted to ease into the school and the community on her own terms, and at the pace she set.

"You don't sound keen."

"I'll be fine." Jaclyn bit her lip.

"My boss, Senior Sergeant Riley Morgan, will be there and he said that the mayor and his wife are coming too."

"Now you've got me worried. It sounds like an event!"

"You'll get used to it. It didn't take me long. Everyone's interested in the school, and keen to hear your ideas."

Jaclyn nodded. "That's great. What I like to hear."

Thalia brought out their coffee and the banana bread they had both ordered and the conversation turned to more general topics. They chatted for a while and Abby glanced at her watch and sighed.

"Sorry I have to rush off, we'll do this again one day soon. We didn't get much of a chance to catch up."

"It's okay. I'm meeting someone else to go and look at a boarding house soon." Jaclyn brushed the crumbs off the loose floral dress that she was wearing. "Oh, while I think of it, I saw something a bit suss at the bridge yesterday. I was going to ring the station on Monday." She recounted what she'd seen and heard, and Abby nodded.

"You're spot on and I know who the two boys are. I'll keep an eye out and have a word if necessary. Thanks Jaclyn. I'll see you Wednesday night, if not before." Abby went to go into the shop, but Jaclyn stopped her.

"My shout. Then we'll have to do it again."

"Thank you, and we will. It's good to have someone around my age in town. I don't fit into the younger set easily. Have a good day."

Jaclyn watched as the paddy wagon cruised slowly up the road.

Chapter 14

"No." Jaclyn shook her head as Lea, the administration manager, sat opposite at the desk in the principal's office on Monday morning clutching a sheaf of invoices. Lea was taking Jaclyn through the school financial procedures. "Absolutely not."

"But that's the way—" Lea's voice held confusion.

The morning had been productive so far; Jaclyn had called a morning muster at 8.30 and met the staff—both high school and primary— and had received a warm and friendly welcome. Following that there had been a brief assembly where she had addressed the students.

When she checked the shared diary that she had placed on the school network, she had been pleased to see that Lea had made and entered three appointments for her after lunch. She was finally beginning to feel like the principal of Bindarra Central School.

She kept her voice pleasant. "Most of the office procedures are excellent, and you've documented them well, Lea."

Lea nodded and the expression on her face lightened a little.

"But there's good reason why the financial procedures I've looked at need to change."

Jaclyn was pleased to see Lea's nod.

"I agree with you, but Kevin wasn't prepared to make the changes I suggested."

"Great," Jaclyn said. "It looks like we're on the same page."

Lea took a deep breath and Jaclyn could see that she was struggling.

Gradually the older woman looked up and held Jaclyn's gaze. "I'd like to apologise for my rudeness to you on Friday. It's no excuse, but I was worried about my husband—he's unwell— and Dave had wound me up. He said that you'd been sent out here as a punishment and I took it personally. I love this town and I love our school and the thought that it would be seen as a punishment by anyone made me angry. I'm very sorry I took it out on you."

Jaclyn nodded and held up her hand. "Wait there." She stood and went over and closed the door. When she'd returned to her desk, she folded her hands on her lap. "Lea, I appreciate your honesty and I'm going to return it." She took a deep breath. "This is very hard for me, and it's the second time I've told this story since I got here. From what you said about Dave's comment and also something I picked up from Helen the cleaner, there's obviously been some mischief done."

Jaclyn's hands were shaking, and she looked down as she gripped them together. "I was assured that my situation was confidential, but I was also told over the weekend that someone is determined to see me fail at Bindarra Creek." She lifted her head and held Lea's gaze steadily. "One thing I will tell you is that I have integrity and I'm honest, and if you hear any of the accusations that have been made, I can assure you that they are entirely false." Another deep breath as her voice shook. "And I will not fail at this school. I'm here to stay and I will do my best to make it the best school it can be."

Lea visibly relaxed. "I believe you, and that's wonderful to hear. We haven't had a principal who cared for a long time. I might be speaking out of line, but you've been honest with me and I appreciate it. Kevin Strickland was an arrogant little shit."

Jaclyn's eyes widened as the older woman swore, and then a smile tilted her lips. "Thank you for *your* honesty."

Lea reached over and held out her hand. "Can we start again please? Welcome to the school, Ms Douglas. It's a pleasure to meet you."

Jaclyn smiled and reached over and took Lea's hand and squeezed it. "Thank you. You don't know how much that means to me, Lea."

"Good. I think we are going to make a good team." Lea's voice was brisk, but she smiled back. "Now tell me how we're going to deal with Kellie and all the personal phone calls she makes?"

In that moment, Jaclyn knew a bond had been forged.

##

An hour later, she looked at Lea. "I think it's time we had a cup of coffee."

Lea giggled. "Do you want Kellie to go and buy you a cream bun?"

Jaclyn stood with a smile. "You're incorrigible, Mrs Kendall!"

The last hour had been emotional as she had recounted the story she'd told to Ryan on Saturday. Lea had been horrified but agreed that the tampering in the system at Sanctuary Garden must have occurred between the coding of the invoices and the cheques.

The existing system at Bindarra Creek totally bypassed the principal in the signing of the cheques as Lea and the deputy were the signatories. Lea had agreed that they needed to change that before any more cheques went out. 'I can see exactly why you made that request, and I agree with your suggestion

163

for the new system.' Lea stood and followed Jaclyn as she opened the door and they both went out into the main office together.

"Kellie?" Lea said with a glance at Jaclyn. 'Has Cleo delivered our morning tea cake yet?'"

Kellie's eyes were wide as she looked from Jaclyn to Lea. "Um . . . Ye…es . . . she has.'

'Good, let's take it down to the staff room and officially welcome our new principal. Ready, Ms Douglas?

Monday and Tuesday followed a similar pattern; the only variation for Jaclyn was packing up to move out of Fig Tree Lodge and into Gemma Haydon's house. Esther Ainslie had taken her around for a visit on Sunday afternoon, and it had been a suitable and more permanent alternative to Fig Tree Lodge. Gemma reminded Jaclyn of Gran, and the conversation had been easy.

"Your meals are included, dear, but I don't expect you to eat with me." Mrs Haydon's smile had been shy, "but if you'd like the company, I'm more than happy to wait my dinner until you get home from school."

Jaclyn had nodded. "Whatever suits you." The room was pretty and spacious and had a small ante-room adjoining the verandah of the low-set Queenslander, that would double as a study.

"And the garage is empty. Since my husband passed away a few years ago, I haven't bothered with a car. You are most welcome to put your car in there."

"And it's close enough to walk to the school. Thank you, Mrs Haydon. I'll take it."

The figure that Gemma mentioned was ridiculously low for board and meals, not to mention a garage for the Audi, and Jaclyn knew she would be very happy to pay more than the requested amount. They arranged for her to move in after school on Tuesday.

Edwina was away for a couple of days, and Jaclyn told Lou at breakfast on Tuesday morning that she would catch up with her when she returned.

"Gemma Haydon is a sweetie," Lou said as she poured Jaclyn's coffee. "And she's a fabulous cook."

"I'll end up putting weight on," Jaclyn said with a smile. "Sitting at a desk all day and eating home cooked meals.'

"You should join the SES," Lou said with a smile. "Ryan Rossiter's joined up already. I believe you're good friends."

Jaclyn spluttered as she sipped her coffee. "Does this town have a gossip radio?" But her smile was light.

"No, we still use smoke signals." Lou's

smile was wide. "To be serious, everyone at the pub on Saturday night saw you and Ryan head to head down at the river, and there's a little bit of gossip around town."

Heat prickled up Jaclyn's neck and she loosened the red scarf that was looped loosely at her throat. "I guess I have to get used to living in a small community." This was very different to how she was used to living. It was a similar sized community to the one Gran had lived in in New Zealand, before she had gone into care. Jaclyn reminded herself of the good things about that. Gran had been happy and told Jaclyn she didn't know what she was missing out on.

"Nothing like fresh air and good people to help when you need a hand." Gran had said. 'I bet you don't even know any of your neighbours in that fancy apartment block of yours."

Jaclyn had shaken her head. "But I'm happy that way, Gran."

"Hmph. We'll see."

But no matter what Gran had said, Jaclyn wasn't sure how she felt about being so visible, and her personal business being known and discussed. In the city she had lived a long way from the schools she'd worked at and had been able to keep her personal life separate.

And that had meant when her career had

taken such a hard hit, she had no one to talk to about it.

"Have you always lived in the city?" Lou interrupted her thoughts as she removed Jaclyn's empty cereal bowl.

"Always, unless you count my teenage holidays with my Gran on a farm in New Zealand."

"I reckon that would count. I hear it's beautiful there. One day when the twins are a bit older, I'd like to see it."

"I'm going over this weekend." Jaclyn put her coffee down and placed the napkin back on the table.

Lou's eyebrows almost reached her hairline. "For a holiday? You've only just started at the school."

'No, just for the long weekend. My grandmother's not well."

"I'm sorry to hear that."

Jaclyn stood and tucked the chair in. "Thanks for looking after me while I've been here at the Lodge, Lou."

"My pleasure, and don't forget we need new members over at the SES. Maybe we'll see you once you get the school settled?"

Jaclyn smiled as she headed back to her room for her suitcase and laptop.

"Maybe."

***

On Tuesday afternoon, Ryan drove back into town from Gunnedah, and he almost broke the speed limit getting back. He was trying hard to reach the school in time to catch Jaclyn before she went home. Over the past two days of meetings and site inspections, his mind hadn't been on his work, as he looked forward to seeing her again; he hoped she wasn't doing it too hard at the school. As he drove past the front gate and went to turn into the school car park, he frowned. It looked like some sort of meeting was happening on the footpath outside the main gate. A small crowd was gathered listening to a man who was shaking his fist and pointing at the school.

A rock lodged in Ryan's stomach. It didn't look good. The car park was full, so he turned around and drove down the road a way and parked next to the oval. He hurried along the footpath just in time to hear the guy yell.

"Who does she think she is anyway? Suspending my son! Now stopping our footie team from playing. I say we vote to get rid of her."

"We don't want a city chick here," a woman called loudly.

He pushed his way through the group and opened the gate and walked towards the front office. Lea and Kellie were standing at the window looking out at the crowd.

Ryan walked across to the counter. "Is everything okay, Lea? Where's Jac—Ms Douglas?"

"In her office. She had to take a call from Sydney." The office manager frowned. "I wonder if I should call the police station. It looks like it's getting nasty out there."

"They're pretty wound up about some kid that got suspended, and a football game."

Lea shook her head and turned back to the window. "I thought I knew him. He seems to be leading the protest. It's the bloke of Parch and Terry doesn't even play in the team."

"He's just shit stirring." Kellie leaned forward. "I think you'd better call, Lea. They're heading through the gate."

Lea hurried to the phone and called over to Ryan. "Can you go down to Jaclyn's office and get her to lock her door. That Parch guy is likely to storm in there. He's already been involved in a few fights in town."

Ryan hurried down the corridor to the principal's office and tapped on the door, before he pushed it open. Jaclyn looked up with a frown and when she looked at Ryan, he could have sworn she looked guilty. He flicked the lock over on the door and walked across to the window and turned his back to give her a bit of privacy.

Jaclyn spoke quietly, but he could hear the tension in her voice. "Thank you, Peter. I'll take that on board, don't worry. I have to go now, there's bit of a situation at the school. I'll talk to you before you get here."

The phone clicked as she put it down and Ryan turned around as Jaclyn stood and walked around the front of the desk to join him at the window.

"Hello, Ryan. What can I do for you?"

"Hello, Jaclyn." For a crazy second it felt natural to lean over and brush her cheek in a greeting, but he pulled himself up in time.

Way unprofessional.

He cleared his throat and shoved his hands in his pockets. "Lea asked me to come in and lock the door. She knew you were on the phone. It's apparently getting a bit nasty out there. What's going on?"

"Just an ordinary day at school with an overreaction by some parents."

"About?" He turned to Jaclyn and her expression softened as he caught her eyes with his.

"The under eighteens football team were heading to a rep game in Tamworth."

"Were?" he asked.

"Until I discovered that there was no paperwork in place, no permission notes and that most of the driving was being done by year 11 students on P plates driving their mates. It's a work, health and safety nightmare."

"And as school manager you're personally liable if anything happens."

"That's right. I've tried to get a minibus but the one from the RSL is in Armidale for the day, and we can't get the normal school buses because they won't be back in time for end of school." She tapped her hand on her thigh as she stared through the window. "Kellie's tried to call the parents to get them to sign permissions notes, but some of them can't get into town. The bottom line is, the paperwork isn't in place for enough boys to make up a team. They are going to have to forfeit.'

"Lea's called the police station to move them on."

"Oh, I don't think that was necessary. I'll go out and speak to them."

"Do you think that's wise?"

"I do. I'm not going to cower in here behind a locked door, Ryan. What sort of impression would that give?"

'Okay, I'll stay close. Where's Deputy Dave?"

Jaclyn snorted. "Ran away with his head down muttering something about my overreaction. He's probably in the bakery by now."

"You've got your work cut out there."

"Yes, he fully expected to get the principal's job so he's white-anting me every chance he gets. There's no need for you to come out." She looked at him and smiled. "Did we have an appointment? How was Gunalda?

"Gunnedah." He grinned back at her. 'You'll have to learn your local towns if you're going to hang around here, Ms Douglas. And no, I just called in to say a quick hello. And to ask you—"

There was a knock on the door, and Jaclyn hurried over to open it.

"It's okay, Jaclyn. Abby was cruising past and she had a word." Lea sounded relieved. "The crowd's dispersed."

"Good, so we can get back to work."

"Yes, but it's going to be raised at the P&C meeting tomorrow night."

"Good, because that was on my agenda too."

Ryan moved to the door as Lea turned and headed back to the office

"What were you going to ask me?"

"If you had time to go for a coffee when school finishes."

"I was going to leave straight after the buses were gone. I'm moving house this afternoon."

"Do you need a hand?"

Jaclyn laughed. "I wasn't very organised when I left Sydney. I only have one suitcase, so thanks, but

I'll be fine." Warmth ran up his arm when Jaclyn reached out and touched his hand. "And I'd love a coffee. The Cyprus Café in half an hour? I have a favour to ask you."

Ryan smiled and it stayed on his face as he headed down to the produce store to fill in the half hour. The Jaclyn of old was gradually coming back as the ice thawed.

Chapter 15

Little tendrils of excitement kept winding their way around Jaclyn's stomach as she tidied her desk ready to leave for the day. She'd been online and booked her return flight to Queenstown for Friday and Monday. Even though it would be a short visit, she'd be able to spend two whole days with Gran. She'd booked a direct flight to Queenstown and had decided to fly to Sydney from Tamworth to save the twelve-hour drive getting to the airport and back. The excitement was because of the trip, she told herself sternly. Or maybe because she was moving into the boarding house this afternoon.

It had nothing to do with the fact that she was about to have coffee with Ryan. Nevertheless, despite what Jaclyn told herself it was still there as she walked to the café. It was strange. Somehow, since their talk and Ryan's kindness to her the other night, their relationship seemed to have gone back to the easiness of old times.

"Hello, Jaclyn." Thalia greeted her as she walked into the café and inhaled deeply. The most glorious combination of coffee, baking meat and sweet pastries filled the air.

"Hello Thalia. What is that wonderful smell?" She peered onto the *bain marie* where a tempting meat dish was keeping warm.

"Ah, that's Mama's Greek spaghetti casserole. Would you like to take some home for your dinner?"

"Thank you, not tonight. Mrs Haydon is expecting me tonight."

"Yes, we heard that you were moving into Wilgara Avenue with her. She's a lovely lady, and a great cook." Thalia lowered her voice and grinned. "Almost as good as Mama, but don't tell anyone I said that."

Jaclyn didn't let the little bristle of annoyance take root. She had to get used to living in a country town.

"I'll take some home please, Thalia." Ryan's warm breath brushed her cheek. "I can recommend it. I've had it about three times since I've been in town."

"More like six, Ryan!" Thalia laughed. "Now can I get you both a coffee?"

Again, Jaclyn realised the grapevine had been working overtime as Thalia seemed to know that they were here together. She nodded. "Thank you."

"The usual?" Thalia asked.

"Yes, please." Ryan pulled out his wallet. "You go and grab a table outside, Jac, and I'll pay for them."

"No, I owe you two coffees."

"You can pay me back later. His voice was warm and held a note that made her toes curl along with her stomach.

Jaclyn smiled her thanks to Thalia and walked outside. The street was quiet. A small girl pushed her way along the footpath on a scooter singing at the top of her voice. About fifty metres behind her, a young woman pushed a pram and struggled with a couple of grocery bags.

"Slow down, Evie. Wait for me on the corner." The woman picked up her pace and smiled at Jaclyn as she walked past.

Jaclyn watched as she caught up to her daughter and they disappeared around the corner. The pace of life was so peaceful here. If she'd been sitting at a coffee shop near her apartment, traffic would have been whizzing past, and the petrol fumes would have necessitated an inside seat. She took a deep breath and her shoulders relaxed as she settled back into the chair.

Bindarra Creek has a lot going for it.

When Ryan came outside, he was juggling two cups of coffee and a plate of pastries.

"Oh yum," Jaclyn said as she took the plate from him.

"You know what, Jac?"

She smiled as he reached over and took a pastry. "What?"

"If for no other reason, this could be why I moved to Bindarra Creek."

"The pastries?"

"Yes." Ryan's next words as he pointed to the street, echoed Jaclyn's thoughts. "And this. The peace and quiet and the slower pace of life."

"Maybe." Jaclyn picked up a sachet of sugar and tipped it into her coffee, aware of Ryan's eyes on her. "It's very different to the city."

"And you know the other thing that I think is great about town?"

"What's that?" she said stirring her coffee.

"The new high school principal."

Heat ran into her face and she looked at him from under her eyelashes. "Flattery is very nice, thank you, but it won't get you your own way on the buildings."

Ryan reached over and picked up her hand. "Trust me, Jaclyn. The buildings are not on my mind at all this afternoon. I'm simply happy you're here. I'm happy you talked to me the other night, and I'm happy that you were happy to have a coffee with me this afternoon."

"Wow, that's a lot of happy," Jaclyn said.

He chuckled and let go of her hand to pick up his coffee.

"It's a big ask, and if you're busy or don't want to, please say no." Jaclyn held his gaze.

"I can't say yes or no until you tell me what you need," Ryan said.

Jaclyn put her cup down and folded her heads in her lap. "Do you remember my gran lives in New Zealand?"

"I do." He nodded.

"She's not been well, and I've decided to go and see her this weekend."

"In NZ?"

"Yes. It's a long weekend."

Ryan's grin was cheeky, and her cheeks heated. "And you'd like company on the trip?"

"Oh no. I didn't mean that." Jaclyn opened her eyes wide and shook her head, embarrassed that Ryan had misunderstood.

"Jac, I'm teasing. What do you need?"

"I was wondering if you could drive me to the airport at Tamworth on Friday afternoon. I don't really want to leave my car at the airport. I know it's a fair drive."

"I'd be happy to. And pick you up on Monday?"

"There's a bus on Monday afternoon. I can wait for that and get the bus back."

"No. I can collect you too. It's less than an hour's drive."

"Thank you," she said softly. "And Ryan?

Thank you being here for me. It's made my move to Bindarra Creek so much easier."

***

"I've always wanted to have a look inside that old building. This town's got some history," Ryan said.

"And it has a ghost too," Jaclyn said as they walked in through the gate. "Edwina's great-granddaughter is named after her."

"Did you see her?"

"No, I've slept through the ghosting hours. I've been tired."

Ryan followed Jaclyn back to Fig Tree Lodge to collect her suitcase, even though she laughed and said it wasn't necessary. It might not have been, but the more time he could spend in her company, the happier he was. Once he'd driven to the boarding house, he parked his ute near the sports ground and waited on the footpath as she drove her Audi into the small shed at the side of the house.

Gemma Haydon looked at him curiously when Jaclyn introduced him as a friend and colleague.

"Would you like to join us for dinner, Mr Rossiter? I've cooked plenty." The elderly woman shook her head with a wry smile. "I still can't get used to cooking for one or two after having a husband and a family."

"Thank you, but I have to get home and look

after my cattle."

"I've heard there's a welcome function after the P&C meeting, Jaclyn. The town's abuzz with coming to meet you."

Jaclyn's fair skin flushed red. "I don't imagine it will be that well attended being a week night."

Mrs Haydon smiled. "You'll be surprised. I've been asked to make a batch of my date scones for supper."

"I'll look forward to them," Ryan said. "I may not need dinner tomorrow night by the sound of things."

"There'll be lots of savoury finger foods too," Mrs Haydon said.

He turned to Jaclyn. "I'll see you at school tomorrow for our meeting, and then I'll be at the P&C Meeting."

"Night, Ryan. And thanks for the coffee. That's three I owe you now." Jaclyn walked to the porch with the elderly woman and waited until he pulled out and headed down the road.

He caught a last glimpse of her as he turned onto the main road. For the first time this week, he wasn't looking forward to going out to his farm and being by himself.

Chapter 16

Jaclyn was quickly discovering that even though she was now principal of a *small* central school, there was still the same amount of work to be done as in a large school. Reports to regional office—the director had called to say he was coming from Tamworth to the P&C meeting tonight—and ongoing data analysis without a large executive staff to delegate the work to, and a constant stream of parents who had issues that would normally have been dealt with by the deputy principal. Deputy Dave had been off 'sick' for two days, which meant a double workload for Jaclyn.

"Dave takes a fair bit of leave," Lea said when she came into Jaclyn's office to tell her he wouldn't be in. The office manager pulled a face. "Most often on Wednesdays when the cattle feed is delivered."

"Cattel feed?" Jaclyn frowned.

"Dave is a farmer first, and a deputy second," Lea answered with a cynical smile.

When Lea went back to the front office, a lengthy—and worrying—call from Peter Hughes had Jaclyn nervous about the upcoming meeting with Ryan. The morning flew by, and before she'd even had time for a lunch break, Lea buzzed to let her know that Ryan had arrived for his appointment.

"Thanks, Lea." Jaclyn rummaged in her drawer—now free of crumbs and cake wrappers and quickly applied a coat of lip gloss and combed her hair. She pulled a face as she put the lipstick and comb away.

What am I doing?

She turned to her computer and tried to look busy as Ryan came down the hall. He paused at the door and Jaclyn gestured for him to come in.

"Take a seat." She pulled the folder containing the buildings documents across in front of her and flicked it open. When she'd spoken to Peter, Jaclyn had taken notes, and circled the areas where she wanted specific answers from Ryan.

Ryan waited for her to start, and she felt a little bit awkward after having spilled her heart to him at the pub on the weekend. She hoped that she could stay professional, but he pre-empted her.

"Jaclyn, this is a professional meeting. Don't look so concerned. We can both be professional and discuss the work issues that we are facing. The issues that we disagree on, and the solution to any problems that you have questions about. Work colleagues when we are in here. Friends when we are out there." He gestured with a nod to the street outside the school.

"Thank you. I'm sure we can." Even though

Peter's call had worried her, she kept her voice light. She would give Ryan a chance to answer her questions honestly, before she wondered if he was on her side

Peter had mentioned Ryan and that had surprised her. "There's a new guy in the Tamworth office and he's sucking up to the community," he'd said. "Apparently, he's moved there and is sweet talking them all into supporting the restoration of the buildings. I'd advise you not to meet with him, and to go to the head of properties in Tamworth for any meetings."

Jaclyn put her hands together on the desk as she read through her notes. She lifted her head and her face heated as Ryan looked at her intently. "Can I begin with some questions?"

"Fire away." He leaned forward and that lock of hair that made him look so cute, fell across his forehead. His work shirt was crumpled, and Jaclyn hid a smile. She knew he hated ironing his shirts, and she wondered if he'd found an ironing person in Bindarra Creek yet. She forced herself to look away as she put her finger on the first line she'd circled.

"It might seem like a strange question, but do you usually visit schools in person? And talk to the communities?"

Ryan reached up and pushed his hair back and his brow wrinkled in a frown. "Yes, that's my job.

My job title is School Liaison Officer."

"Oh. Okay," Jaclyn said slowly. "Someone mentioned that I should go to Tamworth to meet with Properties when there was a big job on, like our buildings."

Ryan shook his head. "No, the point of my job is to save principals making that trek into the regional centre. Sometimes when there are a few of us involved in a project, we might have a videoconference meeting too. And we are aware that your brief is education, and ours is building, so my job is to liaise and advise."

"Okay, just checking the local protocol." Jaclyn cleared her throat. "And what about the community meetings here? Have you had many and can you tell me the mood of the community?" Her voice squeaked and she tried to hide her discomfort. She was *so* out of her comfort zone.

Ryan tipped his head to the side and studied her, and that damn lock of hair fell forward again. Her fingers tingled with the desire to push it back.

"I thought I was here to discuss what we had to do with the buildings? And to agree on what we would say as a team to the community at the meeting tonight. We work for the same department, and we're not on different sides, Jac."

"I know." Jaclyn put one hand up to her mouth before she spoke. "I'm going to be honest with you here, Ryan. It's the way I am, and if it causes issues, so be it. I've had too many experiences lately with people being less than truthful. Someone in state office has warned me about the department out here, and to be frank, he mentioned that you are trying to butter up the community by being on the side of the restoration."

"Who the bloody hell said that?" Ryan's face darkened. "If there's one thing you should know about me, Jaclyn, it is that I have integrity."

"I know you do, and that's why I'm being upfront with you now." Jaclyn sat up straight in her chair. "Why do you think state office are interfering with a local project?"

"I have no idea. It never happened when I worked out of the state office. Who's been talking to you?"

Jaclyn put her head down and bit her lip.

What to do? What to say?

Finally, she sighed. "I shouldn't be reading this to you, because it's got the usual words on the bottom about this email only being for the person it was sent to and all that. It also specifically tells me not to repeat it."

"This is sounding like bullshit to me, Jac."

"I know and I'm sorry. Because of what happened to me in Sydney I have to tread carefully." Jaclyn ran a hand over her eyes.

"Honestly, Ryan, sometimes it all gets too hard and I doubt if this career is the right one for me. I signed up for education, not politics! But this might shed some light on what I'm dealing with. And then after we talk about it, we can decide what we're going to say at the P&C meeting tonight. I'd like us to be on the same page before we go in there."

"Who's it from?"

Jaclyn shook her head and began to read.

"I hope you have already given a great deal of thought to the building situation at BCC and taken my advice seriously. It is essential that the buildings are demolished, and that the advice given by the regional office is not given credence. However, please don't repeat that. It wouldn't create a harmonious relationship."

She paused and looked up at Ryan. His lips were set. "What the—"

"What do you have to say about that?" Jaclyn said calmly.

"I have to say I'm absolutely astounded. That's just plain bullshit." He leaned forward and this time his hand had pushed that recalcitrant lock back before it even fell. "You've seen the buildings now, and you've seen how they are barely damaged structurally. You've heard all about our plans to restore and to make them into specialist rooms." He reached forward and picked up the folder he'd put on the desk. "When I was in Tamworth on Monday, I was given the briefs for the restoration. I didn't want to say anything until I'd read it through, but it's all here, costed, signed off by the director—*in Sydney*—and waiting for you to present it to the community at the P&C meeting tonight."

"In Sydney?" Jaclyn was confused. "And so soon?"

Ryan nodded. "Yes, there was some grant money left over from the last financial year, and our regional office manager put up the proposal that it came to our region, and specifically to Bindarra Creek. Regional office knows how tough the town has done it lately and wanted to contribute. Not only for the restoration of the fire damaged buildings but a renovation—or a rebirth—of the whole school." A smile finally creased Ryan's face. "If you present this to the P&C tonight, you won't have any trouble being accepted by the community."

"I still don't get why Peter—" she cut herself off after his name slipped out.

"Peter?"

Jaclyn shrugged. "The guy from properties in Sydney. You might as well know, we worked together at Sanctuary Gardens High. You never met him."

Ryan's expression was strange. "Is he a really tall guy with salt and pepper hair?"

"Yes, why? Do you know him?"

"No, but I saw you out with him the week you stopped taking my calls. I thought he was your new man."

"What?" Jaclyn's voice was loud as her temper broke. "You assumed that on one sight?"

"Yes." Ryan took a deep breath and looked up at her. "I'm sorry if I hurt you. I guess I was picking up that you'd lost interest in me."

Jaclyn shook her head and struggled to keep her voice even. "This is a conversation for another time. Not here."

"You're right. How about we go through these documents now, and you can see the final ideas." He looked up at her. "And the costings."

Jaclyn stood and heeled her chair around to the other side of the desk. "I'll be able to see better from here as you show me."

"And we'll continue that other conversation after the P&C meeting tonight."

Jaclyn nodded. The expression on Ryan's face filled her with hope.

***

Pride and admiration filled Ryan as he sat in the Bindarra Creek school hall and listened to Jaclyn a few hours later. Every seat was taken by parents and many members of the wider community. Between their meeting in her office and her appearance in the

188

hall, she'd changed her clothes. Her suit was a soft blue, and the matching shoes were high. Ryan forced himself to look away from Jaclyn's legs as she walked across the stage to speak to the assembled crowd after the regional director had formally introduced and welcomed her.

After dealing efficiently with the agenda items, and explaining the WHS requirements for student travel, when Jaclyn moved on to speak of her vision for the school, and her determination to make it the best school in the north west, she was met with enthusiastic applause. He grinned—this was very different to the reception she'd had from the school community on Monday.

To Ryan's surprise, she paused and said there was a special announcement to be made and beckoned him up onto the platform.

"I'm sure many of you have met Ryan Rossiter, another new member of the Bindarra Creek community, and our regional properties liaison officer. Ryan and I had a meeting this afternoon, and there is some news I'd like him to share with you."

Ryan took the steps to the stage two at a time but crossed to Jaclyn first. "This is yours to announce, Jac," he whispered.

She shook her head. "No, this is my way of apologising to you for doubting you. Both professionally and personally. I'm sorry. Ryan."

He took her hand and led her back to the lectern and there were a few murmurs and approving nods from the crowd.

He lifted the microphone. "It's very generous of Ms Douglas to let me make this announcement. We worked together this afternoon, to go over the finer details, and I'm very pleased to say that your new principal has just signed off on the restoration of the high school buildings that were damaged in the fire."

His words were met with a standing ovation, and he couldn't help the pride that filled him as Jaclyn squeezed his hand and didn't let go.

Chapter 17

Jaclyn tried to juggle a plate that was filled with a variety of homemade goodies as Barry Donaldson, the mayor of the district, pounded her back.

"I know you've only been here a short time, Jaclyn—or would you prefer Ms Douglas—but you've done well, and showed you are on the side of our community. He put a whole sausage roll in his mouth, and Jaclyn fought a smile. It was easy to see where that massive girth came from.

"Jaclyn is fine. And thank you. I'm loving being at Bindarra Creek."
And she was. It had been a great evening and she'd forgotten most of the names of the people who had come up and introduced themselves.

Happiness filtered through her, and she turned to speak to the next person waiting to meet her. A tall young man with tight curly black hair, brown eyes, and light brown skin held out his hand. "Hey *dere*! I'm AJ. I'm Barry's son. Welcome to the town. Abby's told me all about you."

Jaclyn fought the eyebrow raise that threatened. She had to get used to country living and country friendliness.

"I work at the station with her," he said.

Ah, the police officer who was sick last weekend when Abby had to work. Jaclyn held out her hand and it was taken in a warm—and tight—grip. "Good to meet you too, AJ."

A warm hand touched her waist and she turned around. Ryan was standing behind her.

"Excuse me, Jaclyn. I was hoping for a quick word."

She introduced AJ to Ryan, and then they left him at the food buffet and walked over to the side of the hall where it was a bit quieter.

"I've never seen so much homemade food in my life," Jaclyn whispered with a smile.

"I don't need dinner, that's for sure," Ryan said. "But I was going to ask you to come to the pub with me. I wanted to finish our conversation."

Jaclyn nodded. She spoke quietly. "Why don't you come back to my place. I have a small living room off the bedroom, and I've already set up my coffee maker."

"Have you been shopping at the electrical store already?" Ryan asked with a grin. "You and your coffee!"

Jaclyn smiled. "No, I brought it with me from my apartment. It was the first thing I thought to pack when I got moved out here. I didn't need it at Fig Tree Lodge because the coffee there was excellent. Please don't tell Gemma I said this"—she looked around guiltily, her landlady was here somewhere— "but Nescafe instant doesn't quite reach the mark for me."

"You're a coffee snob, Jac," he said but his voice was teasing.

"And proud of it," she replied. "Would you like to call in and have a real coffee on your way home."

"Are you allowed to have a gentleman guest?"

She couldn't help the giggle that bubbled up. "I'm not in a convent, Ryan. I'm merely renting a room."

"But you're in a small town, and you have a reputation to uphold." He nudged her with his elbow, and the warm sizzle ran right down to her—

Ryan took her arms with both hands and pushed her gently towards the crowd. "Now go and mingle some more. There's still a lot of people waiting to meet you. I'll help Lea and the P&C ladies clean up, and I'll walk you home. I didn't see your car in the car park, so I assumed you walked. And yes, I'd love to see your new place and have a coffee. And finish what we were talking about."

Anticipation fired in Jaclyn's stomach, and she pushed away the warm feeling that was building. "Okay, I'll see you in half hour or so."

##

The sky was clear and the air still as Ryan waited outside the main office block. Jaclyn had set

193

the alarms to the hall and had gone back to the office to get her bag and check that everything was locked up securely. Ryan had listened as the mayor had spoken at the supper about the arsonist who had caused damage in the town a couple of months ago, and he could understand why Jaclyn was careful about locking up.

The lights went out, and he heard the door open. A whiff of Jaclyn's fresh floral perfume preceded her and when she reached him, he held out his arm. She crooked her hand through his elbow. Relief rushed through Ryan; despite Jaclyn being friendly and warm to him all evening, he was still worried about the discussion they'd had this afternoon.

He knew her trust had been damaged by the experience that she had had in Sydney, but it hurt to know that she had doubted him. Her fingers were warm against the inside of his arm, and he fought back the rush of desire that came from that simple touch.

"That was a very successful night, Ms Douglas," he said to change the directions of his thoughts. All he wanted to do was pull Jaclyn close and kiss her. The first time he'd kissed her since they'd had their last weekend away.

She moved closer to him as they walked towards the gate and Ryan bit back the groan that threatened.

"It was. And you know what?" She turned her head to face him as they walked.

"What?" He cleared his throat.

"I enjoyed myself. Once we got the formal stuff over and I started to meet people, it made me realise that this is a great place. Everyone is pulling together and really happy about the buildings being restored."

"Are you?" he asked quietly.

"I am. I trust you, Ryan, and I'm going to get to the bottom of this stuff with Peter. But that's enough of that. School's over for the day and we have some talking to do."

She held onto his arm as they left the school grounds and walked past the sports oval. "Gemma's gone out for the night. Apparently, this is her card night. It was good of the rest of them to come."

"For a small town, there's a lot to keep you occupied." He nudged her. "If you ever take any time off school to do it, that is."

"Hey, this is the new me."

They reached the front gate of Gemma Haydon's house and the large tree inside the fence blocked the light from the front porch.

Ryan stopped walking when they reached the shadows and took Jaclyn's other arm. He turned her around and put his hands on her waist. "I don't know if I want a new Jaclyn. Did I ever tell you how much I liked the old one?"

Her smile was wide as she looked up at him, and Ryan knew there was much more than 'like' involved. "You did? I'm sorry Ryan I'm sorry for the way I treated you all those months ago."

He lowered his head and rested his forehead against hers. "Hey, Jac. It was a two-way street. If I hadn't jumped to the wrong conclusion when I saw you with that guy, I would have persevered when you didn't take my calls. If I had, I would have been there for you when you went through all that garbage with the department."

She moved her head so that her cheek was resting against his and Ryan closed his eyes.

"It's okay. We're here now . . . together."

"Are we together again? Do you mean that the way I'm hoping you are?"

The slight nod against his cheek filled him with happiness.

"If you still want me, it does."

Ryan put his finger beneath Jaclyn's chin. He didn't care that they were standing near a public street in the middle of a small town. All he could think of was the feel of the woman in his arms. The woman who was now looking up at him with warmth in her eyes.

"As much as I tried to convince myself that we weren't right for each other, I never stopped loving you, Jac."

He felt her jerk in his arms, and he tightened his hold. "I might be going too fast, but I loved you then, and I love you even more now. I'm not going to waste any more time. We've wasted enough time. I've waited too long to tell you that."

He lowered his head and those sweet familiar lips opened beneath his as Jaclyn murmured against them. "We have, but it was worth the wait."

Once they were inside, they talked until it was almost midnight, and Gemma's key rattled in the front door. Ryan held Jaclyn close on the sofa as she lay back on him and rested her head on his chest. He dropped a kiss on her hair.

"It's time I was going. I've got an early start tomorrow. A ten o'clock meeting in the office in Tamworth."

"I'd like to offer you a bed, but I don't think it would be the right thing to do on my second night in the boarding house."

Ryan chuckled. "We could get a motel room."

"The motel is owned by one of my school parents. I met her tonight."

Ryan tapped his chin and looked down at Jaclyn. "So I guess, to stop the town gossip mill working overtime, you're going to have to come out and spend the weekends at my place."

"Is that an invitation?" Her voice was coy, but

her eyes were dancing.

"It sure is."

"Don't forget you're driving me to Tamworth on Friday and I'm away for the whole weekend."

"I haven't forgotten. So how about the following weekend?"

Jaclyn didn't speak, but when she reached up and pulled his head down to meet her lips, Ryan knew that was a yes.

A long and most satisfactory yes.

Chapter 18

Jaclyn woke bright and early the next morning. Her mood was still zinging from last night; it had been hard to say goodbye to Ryan. It was as though they hadn't had the six months apart and knowing that he was going to be here in Bindarra Creek as she settled into her new school kept the smile on her face. Even the thought of going to work made her happy; things were working out well at school. The only downside was that comment that Peter had made about someone being out to get her, and a lazy deputy principal. Jaclyn shrugged; she was a long way from the politics of Sydney, and she would keep a very close eye on the finances and grants. Gemma had left out cereal and milk and Jaclyn had a quick breakfast. The coffee could wait until she got to school. She pulled the front door shut quietly—Gemma had told her she was a late riser—and walked the short distance to the school. It was a clear and warm morning, and she welcomed the anticipation of the day ahead.

Lea was already in the office and looked up as Jaclyn walked in the main door.

"Morning, Lea. How's your husband?"

"Much better, thank you. The new treatment seems to be working."

"That's great news."

The phone rang and Jaclyn walked over to pick it up. "Good morning, Bindarra Creek Central School."

"I would like to speak to the principal please."

"Peter?"

"Yes, is that you Jaclyn? I thought you'd be there already. Listen I'm only about an hour out of town, on my way to Tamworth. I was wondering if you'd left yet or if you'd like a lift to the meeting at the regional office with me." He chuckled. "But you obviously haven't left yet."

"Meeting? What meeting is that?"

"You were cced into the email yesterday afternoon. A properties meeting."

"I haven't got to my email yet. I was at a P&C meeting last night. Give me a moment and I'll check and call you back."

"Don't worry about calling back. I'll drop into the school on my way through town."

"Okay. I'll come with you as long as you're coming back straight after the meeting?"

"I am. I have to be back in Sydney tonight." Peter's tone was more formal than usual. "I've been invited to represent the department at a function where the Premier is speaking."

Hmm, meteoric rise up the greasy pole, Jaclyn thought.

"Good, there's a couple of things I want to talk to you about. We can talk on the way."

Lea looked her curiously as she put the phone down. "You're heading out? A problem?"

"Sorry?" Jaclyn looked at her distractedly.

"You look worried."

"No. All good. A colleague from Sydney is calling in and apparently there's a meeting in Tamworth I'm required at this morning. It's short notice but I think I'd better go. Do we know yet if Dave's in today?"

"He said he'd be back today."

"Good. I'll just go and clear my email and see what this meeting's all about."

Jaclyn frowned as she walked to her office, opened the door and crossed to her desk. She booted up the desktop computer and logged on, feeling guilty that she hadn't checked her email last night.

She'd been too busy being kissed senseless by Ryan. A smile played about her lips and she made up her mind that she wouldn't let Peter Hughes upset her. The buildings had been signed off without his intervention.

But she was going to speak to him and get to the bottom of what he knew about the situation in Sydney, and the strange warning that he'd given her.

Her email program opened and sure enough, there was an email from the local director requesting her to attend the meeting at ten o'clock this morning in Tamworth. She hadn't spoken to him much at the supper last night. Rob Jones had a quick cup of tea and left soon after, but it was strange that he hadn't mentioned it. It must be the same meeting that Ryan had mentioned.

Jaclyn shrugged. She would have to go.

An hour later, Lea buzzed her. "Your visitor has arrived."

Jaclyn went out to the foyer.

Peter Hughes was a tall man and he had presence. His once dark hair was peppered with grey, and he exuded a sense of self-importance. When they'd first worked together, she'd found his physical size almost intimidating, but soon realised that it wasn't accompanied by a strong personality. It was a good thing that he was out of a school position; Peter was much better suited to an office job, rather than dealing with students and parents on a daily basis.

Jaclyn held out her hand and tried not to recoil when Peter leaned in and kissed her cheek. Lea caught her eye and raised her eyebrows before looking down.

Jaclyn stepped back, and her voice was cool.

"Please come down to my office, Peter."

He looked at his watch and shook his head. "We really don't have much time. Let's talk in the car on the way. It really is critical that we get to this meeting. It's about your buildings. I told you not to trust that Rossiter bloke."

This time Lea's eyes were wide as she switched her gaze back to Peter.

"I'll fill you in as we go."

"Let me get my bag." Jaclyn turned to Lea. "Can you please let Dave know he's in the chair today?"

Lea nodded. "I saw him drive into the car park while you were talking."

"Good. I'll be back as soon as the meeting is over. Any dramas, tell him to call my mobile."

Jaclyn collected her bag and followed Peter out to the road where he'd parked the white department station wagon in the bus zone. Opening the door, he waited as she climbed into the passenger seat. He nodded towards the school and for a moment it sounded like glee in his voice.

"Bit of a comedown from Sanctuary Gardens, Jaclyn?"

"It's a very good school, and I'm pleased to be here." Jaclyn counted to ten as he walked around and opened the driver's door and climbed in.

Peter started the car and pulled away from the

kerb without speaking again, and Jaclyn tried to think of the best way to broach the questions she wanted to ask. As they approached the first intersection, Peter slowed down and then drove across Main Road.

"You should have turned left there, Peter," she said.

"Sorry. I missed the turn. I'm worried about the things I have to tell you." His voice was tense, and Jaclyn shot him a glance.

"Take a right at the next corner and if you go around the block, it'll get us back onto the main road."

"Bloody hell. Give me the city any day." Peter yawned as he peered ahead. "At least you get road signs there."

"Are you okay, Peter? What time did you leave Sydney to get here so early?"

"I stayed in Tamworth last night."

Jaclyn looked at him curiously. "So why did you come back to Bindarra Creek if you were already there?"

"Because I really need to talk to you . . . before the meeting. And I thought I could look at the building, but I misjudged the time it took me to get here. Bloody country roads."

"Take the next right," Jaclyn said as she pointed to the next intersection. "I want to talk to you too."

He followed her directions and turned onto Main Street.

"Next right and then straight ahead and you're on the Tamworth Road." She was getting to know her way around the town streets.

"I know. I came in this way." Peter looked ahead and his lip curled. "What a sad little town. How can you stand it? Three years you have to stay?"

"Leading a school is the same wherever you might be. And that's why I'm here." Jaclyn burred up. "It might look a bit dry at the moment, but that's the drought that has much of the country in its grip. The town is a lovely place and I've been made very welcome by everyone."

Peter's chuckle held disbelief. "You don't have to pretend to me that you're happy here, Jaclyn. And you're only here because you stuffed up big time."

"There's no pretence in it, Peter. Granted it's a smaller school, but I've already enjoyed my first few days more than my six months at Sanctuary Gardens. And as far as the stuffing up comment, you don't know what you're talking about."

"You'd be very surprised what I know. You're just kidding yourself that you'll be content here. I give you six months tops."

"You don't know me well enough to know what

I like and what I want."

"You'd be surprised what I know about you. And I do know what happened. More than you ever could have guessed."

Jaclyn shot him an icy glare. She'd forgotten how rude Peter could be and was already regretting accepting the lift with him. "You said in your email the other day that you knew I was innocent of any wrong doing."

"Did I?"

"Yes, you did, and there's a few other things you mentioned that I'd like to know what you were talking about."

Peter slowed the car and put the indicator on, but Jaclyn was focused on her determination to get to the bottom of what he'd said in his email.

"What did you mean the other day when you said you knew who it was who set me up, and that they are still determined to see me fail here?" Jaclyn's voice shook as the injustice of her situation overwhelmed her. She'd been so busy at school over the past few days, she'd managed not to dwell on the events that had brought her to Bindarra Creek. She clasped her hands together and took a deep breath.

"And what are you going to do if I tell you who it was that interfered with the school finances?"

"I'll be taking it straight to the department and

making sure that my name is cleared."

"Jaclyn." Peter shook his head. "You really aren't politically savvy, are you? I don't know how you ever got to be a principal." His voice was smug.

"What do you mean by—." Jaclyn looked out the window as the car hit a rough patch of road, and she frowned. They had turned off the main road to Tamworth and were on a dirt road.

"Why did you turn off the main road?" As she asked, they passed a group of children in Bindarra Creek uniforms waiting at a bus shelter where the main road intersected with two dirt roads. She caught a brief glimpse of Terry Parch smoking as they sped past.

That'd be right.

"Don't stress. That was always your problem. You're a control freak, Jaclyn. You always have to know what's going on." Peter's tone held patience as though he was speaking to a child. "It's a back road, and a quicker way to Tamworth." He glanced at his watch. "We've only got an hour to get there."

"It's only forty-five minutes by the main road." Jaclyn folded her arms. "So what did you mean by politically savvy?"

"We're well on the way on this shortcut now. I'll keep going this way. And what I meant was, you never understood the politics of the department."

"I'm an educator Peter. First and foremost the

welfare and learning of the students was—and is—
my priority

He shook his head. "Like I said, you have no
idea."

Jaclyn tried to relax. What Peter said was true;
maybe wanting to be in control all the time wasn't
such a good habit. As she'd grown up and was
dumped on Gran every school holiday break, Jaclyn
soon realised that her father didn't care what she
did. So at sixteen years of age she'd taken control of
her life, and her decision-making; that's why the
situation at Sanctuary Gardens had hit so hard when
she'd had no way to overcome or control over what
had happened to her career.

He glanced over at her as the car hit a bump.
"Same as with this building program. You have to
listen to me. You want to look good at this new
school? You have to fight this restoration."

Jaclyn sensed if she told him that she'd already
signed off on the restoration she would get very
little out of him. He'd find out soon enough when
they got to the meeting in Tamworth. Once he knew
that she'd get nothing out of him.

"Okay I'll take onboard what you're saying."

"Good." He nodded crisply. The tension had
dissipated a little.

"So, Peter. Tell me about your new job," Jaclyn
asked. "Are you on secondment or have you moved

across to the city office for good?"

"Are you really interested or are you making conversation?" he asked as he hit the brakes.

Jaclyn glanced through the window. The road was deteriorating the further they went. "I'm interested," she said quietly. "I know that being a deputy principal wasn't something that you wanted to do or got much pleasure from, Peter."

"Well, you've nailed that," he said as he changed back a gear. "I wanted to be principal, but no, they had to appoint a woman over me. I knew that school, and that job should have been mine."

A glimmer of unease settled in Jaclyn's chest and she frowned. Before she went to speak, Peter slammed on the brakes again as the road ahead turned in a hundred- and eighty-degree switchback.

"For God's sake, Peter, what is this road?"

"Welcome to the country," he said with a smarmy smile. "Get used to it."

"Are you sure you know where you're going? Is this the way you came over from Tamworth?"

"Hmm. I may have turned off too soon."

"Well, I suggest you turn around and go back to the main road."

"And I suggest you stop trying to tell me what to do! You don't like being out of control, do you, Jaclyn? Well it's your turn now. What goes around comes around, they say." Peter changed back a gear

as they approached another switchback, and Jaclyn
gripped the sides of the seat as the station wagon
sped down the steep hill. "Don't worry, we'll reach
our destination very soon."

Chapter 19

Ryan arrived at the office with an hour to spare before the ten o'clock meeting. He checked his email and made a coffee before he went over and knocked on his boss's door.

"Come in, Ryan." Ron Perkins was sitting at his desk, frowning at the computer screen. His frown was a frequent sight in regional office, and cause for much teasing. Only a few months from retirement, Ron was known for his old-fashioned preference of working with pen and paper, and had to be reminded to keep up to date with his emails.

"Need a hand, Ron?" Ryan asked as he walked across to the desk.

"What do you think? Someone sent me this thing with the message, and I have no idea how I'm supposed to read it."

"An attachment?"

"I don't know what you call it, it's got a paper clip thingy next to the message."

"Beats me how you ever got to be boss, Ron," Ryan said as he clicked on the attachment and a pricing spreadsheet opened on the screen. Within seconds the printer was whirring, so Ron could hold it and read it on paper.

"Because I'm bloody good at my job," Ron replied with a grin. "Some of you young blokes place way too much importance on those things." He gestured to the computer on his desk. "What happens when the electricity fails, and you have to think for yourselves? In the good old days . . ." He shook his head. "Anyway, what can I do for you?"

Ryan picked up his coffee and it burned his tongue as he sipped it. "How much do you know about the staff at state office?"

"Know what about them?"

"It's to do with the work at Bindarra Creek?"

Ron nodded. "Nothing to do with state. It's a regional project."

"That's what I thought. How much input did state office have in the decision making about the building restoration?"

"None," Ron said. "It's a local issue. And we have our regional budget. You know that, don't you?"

"I thought I did, but someone in the Sydney office has been interfering in the program, and emailing Jaclyn Douglas with advice. It's a bit strange. I thought I was right because when I worked in Sydney, the state office had very little, if anything, to do with the various district offices. Even in the Sydney district office we looked after our allocated schools and had little contact with the state office in town."

"Yep. And that's how it works in regional New South Wales too. What sort of interference are you talking about?"

"An officer telling the new principal that regional office has no 'credence', I think was the word used, and that I was trying to butter up the community by being on the side of the restoration."

Ron shook his head. "I think you'd better hand this over to me. It sounds very strange indeed. Who is it saying this?"

"I don't know his last name, but it's Peter something, and apparently he's a deputy principal who's been seconded to state office from a high school."

Ron picked up the phone with a frown. "I'll go straight to the horse's mouth, and if this is true, I'll be giving state a huge serve. One minute they're all for decentralisation to save government money, and in the next breath they want control again."

Ryan stood to leave, but Ron waved him back to his seat. "Stay there, I might have some questions for you."

He sat down again and waited.

"Jim, how goes it?" Ron's voice was loud. "Yep, all good out here except for the bloody drought."

Ryan stared at the wall as the conversation

covered personal topics for a few minutes.

"Okay, Jim. I've got a meeting in a quarter of an hour, and I need some answers first. Apparently one of your properties officers has been sticking his nose in a program at one of our schools. There's a new principal just taken over and it's caused some confusion."

Ron nodded as he listened. "Bindarra Creek," he finally said. "Where the fire was. We've just signed off on the building restoration yesterday. Your bloke's been questioning the decision, I believe." Again, a pause. "Yes, I know and that's why I'm ringing. Peter someone. He's been seconded to you from the north shore. Sanctuary Gardens High." Ron picked up the pages he'd printed out, obviously waiting for an answer. After a long minute he spoke. "Listen, Jim. Do you want to ring me back?" He tapped his fingers on the papers and frowned. "Okay, well that is bit strange, but fair enough. I didn't think anyone would interfere with the way we run things out here. And Jim, don't forget that offer's still open for a golfing weekend."

Ryan sat straight and stared at his boss, keen to hear what was going on.

Ron put the phone down and scratched his head as he stared at Ryan. "Tell me about Jaclyn Douglas. Would she have an agenda of her own here? Any reason to make this up?"

214

Ryan shook his head, keen to defend Jaclyn's name. "No, of course not. I'm absolutely sure of that. She was happy to sign off on the papers last night, and we announced it to the school community at a P&C meeting last night. Why, what's wrong?"

Ron screwed his face up. "Someone's telling porkies. There's no Peter in properties at state office, and Jim laughed when I said he'd been seconded. There's a staffing freeze on."

##

The ten o'clock meeting ran over time, and it was after twelve by the time that Ryan got back to his office. He picked up his phone to call Jaclyn and then put it down again. It would be better to get to the bottom of this in person. After last night, and what a happy night they'd had, the last thing he wanted was for Jaclyn to think that he doubted her.

Or that she was lying.

He hadn't entertained that idea for one moment. Ryan tried to remember the words of the email that she'd read to him the other day as he drove into Bindarra Creek in the early afternoon. He hit speed dial for the school.

Kellie picked up the phone straight on the first ring. "Bindarra Creek Central School. How may I help you?"

Ryan grinned. In less than a week, he'd seen an improvement in Kellie's professionalism. Jaclyn was already making a difference to the school.

"Hey, Kellie. It's Ryan. I'm just driving into town, and I wanted to know if Jaclyn had any free time for an appointment later this afternoon."

"Would you please hold the line while I check Ms Douglas's electronic diary."

Ryan slowed the car as he crossed the bridge. A couple of teenagers in school uniform ran across the road and under the bridge on the north side.

"Ya still there?" Kellie asked.

"Yep, I'm here."

"Ms Douglas has a spot free at three, but she's out at a meeting, and we don't know how long she'll be."

"Okay, thanks, Kellie I'll call later. I have to go out to Willingham School, so I'll check in before I leave there." It would be quicker to cut back across to his property without going back to town, but if Jaclyn was back in time he'd make the effort.

Then again, even if she wasn't back in time to meet with her at the school, maybe he'd come via town anyway and suggest going to the Riverside pub for dinner. Ryan was happy that Jaclyn was going to visit her grandmother, but it was a shame it was this weekend, just when they'd got themselves sorted.

He reached over to flick the radio on with a smile.

There'd be many more weekends to spend together.

Chapter 20

Jaclyn let go of the breath she'd been holding as they came off the dirt road. It changed to tar and they passed over a crossroad. The signpost indicated it was only twenty kilometres to Tamworth.

"See, I told you I knew what I was doing." Peter accelerated along the bitumen and the car picked up speed. "Now what was it you wanted to know?"

"Who it was that changed the codes of the invoice payments?"

"Ah, that's right. We were talking about your political astuteness. Do you realise that even though the truth has come out, it won't mean anything for you?"

"What truth?"

"I've got my ear to the ground. They know it wasn't you, and the person responsible has been dismissed. Very quietly."

"So how do you know all this in state office, and why haven't I been told?"

"Do you really have to ask that? Think, Jaclyn. You're not a stupid woman. Is the department going to put themselves in a position where you could sue for wrongful demotion? Of course they're not.

They've already lost fifty grand in the stuff up that you didn't see coming even though it was your school. They're not going to risk a big payout to you too."

"I thought you said they'd dismissed the person responsible." Jaclyn chewed at her bottom lip. It had to be someone on the staff at Sanctuary Gardens, she thought. But she'd been over that possibility on many sleepless nights, and not had any ideas.

"They have dismissed them, but they didn't get the money back. So I suggest that you settle out here quietly in your little country town and try to toe the line if you ever want to get back to the city."

"Toe the line?"

"Insist that these buildings be demolished."

"I'm curious, Peter. You haven't seen the buildings for yourself, have you?"

"No."

"So how do you know it's the right thing to do?"

"Jaclyn, Jaclyn."

She tensed as Peter took his eyes from the road and looked at her and then shook his head.

"It's not about doing the right thing. It's about how it will make you look."

"That's a very selfish and cynical viewpoint." Jaclyn sat up straight. "I'll be interested to sit in on this meeting. Region obviously haven't kept you up to date with the progress out here."

"What progress?" His eyes narrowed and he slowed the car.

"I signed off on the restoration yesterday and it was announced to the community last night at the P&C meeting. And the regional director was there and he was very happy that I agreed, as was the Bindarra Creek community. So I guess that you've been invited to this meeting as a courtesy to state office."

Peter slammed the brakes on and swung the car to the right and onto a narrow dirt road. "You stupid bitch! That's not the way it was supposed to happen."

He floored the accelerator and the bushes along the side of the road scraped against the car.

"Where are you going now?"

"Just shut up and let me think."

"Think about what?" Jaclyn glanced through the window as the road narrowed to little more than a track. A small creek ran below a steep drop, and the edge of the track had subsided in places. "You're going to have to turn around, Peter."

"Don't tell me what to do," he yelled.

"Calm down."

"I won't bloody calm down. You've ruined everything."

Jaclyn clung to the seat as her side of the car tipped briefly before the tyres grabbed the road again. "I don't understand why you're so upset."

"How about I tell you, and then you can get out and walk."

"Get out and walk where?"

"I don't give a rat's arse where you go." He turned the engine off and Jaclyn frowned as the lock on her door snicked loudly. "Before you get out and find your own way home, I'll tell you what I'm so upset about." Even though he'd turned the car off, Peter still gripped the steering wheel so tightly his fingers were white.

For the first time, a glimmer of fear shimmied through Jaclyn. She calmed herself by taking in a deep breath. Peter had obviously lost the plot, and if she had to find her way back, she would.

"You came into Sanctuary Gardens and took the job that was supposed to be mine. The golden-haired girl. My God, they were even talking about you being a director one day." His laugh held no mirth. "But we both know that would never have happened. I've got more political savvy in my little finger than you'll ever have. So I made sure you looked bad."

"You did?" Her eyes widened in disbelief as the truth stared her in the face. "It was you all along?"

"How else would I know what happened, duh?

And I made a nice fifty grand on the side." Peter smiled. "You're not real smart and you'll bring yourself down eventually. Even in your 'wonderful little country town.'"

"You bastard! And all the time you spent sitting in my office sympathising with me!"

"I enjoyed those little meetings we had," he said. "You spilled your heart, didn't you, sweetheart?"

"But what are you doing in state office? You said they—*you*—had been dismissed. Is that another lie?"

"No, that's the truth."

"But what about your job in properties?"

"I said that so you would listen to me. I know how much they wanted this restoration, and it you'd refused to agree with it, you would have looked like even more of a fool." He laughed. "You probably would have been shipped further west."

He unlocked the door and Jaclyn clutched her bag, keeping a wary eye on Peter. "So there was no meeting in Tamworth?"

"No."

"But what about this government car, and you were emailing me from a department account."

"Get out." Peter gestured with his head, but Jaclyn stayed where she was.

"Answer me."

"But what about the government car?" he parroted her words. "It's a white station wagon, sweetheart, I've had it for a couple of years. And any fool can set up an alias, so the account looks like it comes from the department. Now get out. It's enough for me that you've ended up out in this godforsaken bush."

"How am I going to get back to Bindarra Creek?"

"Well, Jaclyn, I don't give a flying you-know-what. Now get out before I shove you down that creek bank."

Clutching her bag in her right hand, Jaclyn opened the door and climbed out. She slammed the door shut, pleased to be away from Peter's toxic words. He revved the car up the track spraying her with clods of dirt as the wheels spun.

"Well, that was fun," she muttered under her breath. She was still furious at what Peter had disclosed, and fear hadn't had time to push in. As she looked around, her predicament came home to her.

Here she was mid-morning, in the middle of bush that she was unfamiliar with. All she knew was that the last sign post had said twenty kilometres to Tamworth, but that had been a while ago. Opening her bag, she dug around checking she still had the bottle of water that was usually in there.

Relief flooded through her as her fingers closed around the narrow neck of the plastic bottle. And at the same time brushed against the muesli bar that she'd packed for morning tea today.

At least she wouldn't starve or get dehydrated. And if the worst came to the worst, this creek had followed the road for a while, and she could top up her water.

Jaclyn dug deeper into the side pocket of her bag and pulled out her phone. As she had expected there was no service. She stood there for a few minutes looking at her surroundings, and remembering that she hadn't noticed one farmhouse, nor had they passed another car on the way in. Behind her—the way Peter had driven in— were acres and acres of bush, and no sign of life. She could walk all day and end up in a place like she was in now.

She turned and looked in the direction that Peter had gone; he had either known that the road led somewhere or had merely expected that it would go somewhere. She took a few steps in that direction and was pleased to see that the road forked and there was an old sign post. Hurrying along to the spot, she squinted trying to read the faded words.

To the left Tamworth was thirty-five kilometres. To the right Mt Yarrie was six kilometres. From where she was she could see a trig station on the peak.

Jaclyn stood there and tried to breathe calmly. She was on a road, and surely someone would come along eventually if she stayed on it and didn't venture into the bush and get lost. It was hours until it would get dark, and there was a low covering of cloud so it shouldn't get too hot.

As she pondered her dilemma she glanced down at her phone and then up at Mt Yarrie looming in the near distance. If she got to the top of the mountain there was a good chance there would be a phone signal.

If she got up there and there wasn't, well she'd just have to turn around and come back down again; it was downhill all the way back to the road.

All she had to do was stay on the road, watch out for snakes and wildlife, and if she heard Peter coming back, she'd go bush.

The thought of going into that long brown grass made her shiver, but Jaclyn knew that things could have been be a lot worse. She could still be locked in the car with Peter travelling to goodness knows where. She was having trouble processing what he'd told her. It was hard to understand someone holding such a grudge that he would go to those lengths to get back at her. The unfairness of her situation twisted in her, like a knife turning in her chest. Jaclyn knew what Peter had said about clearing her name was true; she had seen the department in action with staff on stress leave. She didn't want compensation; she wanted her reputation restored.

Something cool ran down her cheek and she lifted her hand, and looked at her damp fingers.

Tears? Pull yourself together, Jaclyn.

Impatiently she scrubbed at her cheeks and then set off determinedly for the road that led to the top of the mountain.

I am fit enough and I can do it.

But as she approached the fork in her road, the sound of a car coming towards her broke the still morning air and she held her breath.

It was the road that Peter had driven along; he wasn't coming back to help her. With a strangled cry Jaclyn ran for the low scrubby bush and dived into the undergrowth as the white station wagon sped around the corner.

The sandy soil shifted beneath her shoes. Jaclyn desperately grabbed for a hand hold as her feet slipped down the steep incline, but there was nothing there.

She gasped as the huge drop loomed below. Holding back the scream that rose in her chest she lurched forward as gravity pulled her down into the void.

Chapter 21

Ryan hadn't got back into town last night as Ron had called him at Willingham School; by the time he'd used their videoconference facility so that he and the principal could talk to Ron together, it had been too late to drive back to Bindarra Creek. A couple of times on the way home he'd tried Jaclyn's mobile, but it had gone to voice mail, and he'd left a message.

Hope you had a good meeting, love you.xxx

His finger had hovered over the keys, but he'd held off adding any more. The conversation about her ex-deputy's con was one for a face-to-face chat.

Jaclyn hadn't called back. Feeling a little deflated, Ryan cooked a frozen beef burger on the barbeque and had an early night.

He whistled as he parked his ute in the school car park at eight o'clock the following morning. Lea's small sedan was in her usual spot, but he knew that Jaclyn's Audi would be safely parked in the shed at the boarding house. Anticipation surged through him. It might be unprofessional, but if he closed Jaclyn's office door he could steal a quick good morning kiss. He climbed out of the ute and opened the gate to the school. Glancing across at the charred weatherboards Ryan nodded, very pleased with the outcome. He'd have to spend time at the school overseeing the work as the buildings were restored and fitted out into specialist rooms.

"Morning, Lea."

The office manager looked up with a wide smile as he came in juggling two coffees from the Cyprus Cafe. "You're bright and early this morning, Ryan."

"And you're looking very bright and happy." Not only was there a wide smile on Lea's face, but she'd had her hair coloured and ditched the usual grey cardigan for a red shirt.

"I am. We celebrated and Cleo and Jon came over. David's got the all clear."

"That's great news."

"It's a huge relief. The next step was going to be some time in hospital in Sydney, but everything's good now. Are you here to see Jaclyn?" She sent him a knowing look and Ryan grinned. Small town gossip was in action.

"Yes." He held up the coffee. "I'll take it down to her office."

"She's not arrived yet, but I'm sure she won't be long. It's late for her, and she didn't come back after her meeting in Tamworth yesterday. She must have had a long day."

"Tamworth?" Ryan frowned. "I didn't realise

her meeting was in Tamworth. I was there all morning and I didn't see her car there."

"No, she got picked up by that fellow from Sydney."

Ryan's blood chilled and he carefully placed the two takeaway cups on the counter. "What fellow from Sydney?"

Lea looked at him with a frown. "She said he was a colleague from Sydney."

"Did you get his name?"

"I heard her call him Peter, but that's all I know."

"Shit." Ryan pulled out his mobile and called Jaclyn, but it went straight to voicemail. "Lea, can you call Gemma and ask her to see if Jaclyn is home? I've got a bad feeling about this."

Lea picked up the phone and dialled, and spoke to Ryan as she waited. "What sort of bad feeling?"

"I found out yesterday that this bloke who's been emailing Jaclyn isn't with the department anymore."

"But they were going to a meeting." She turned to the phone. "Hi Gemma, it's Lea. I was wondering if you could tell me if Jaclyn's on her way to school yet." She paused. "What? Okay. Thanks for that." She stared at Ryan. "She didn't come home last night, but Gemma didn't worry. She thought that Jaclyn must have gone out to your place." Lea's face had paled. "He said they were going to a meeting and that they had to hurry."

"That's what *he* said, but they weren't at the properties meeting I went to in Tamworth yesterday."

"Ryan?" Lea's voice was hesitant. "Um, I don't want to be a gossip, but I think you need to know."

"Yes?"

"That Peter kissed Jaclyn when he arrived yesterday."

"No, that's nothing to worry about." Ryan shook his head. "I know Jaclyn and I would trust her with my life. If he did, it wasn't something she would have wanted. We need to report her missing and then I'm going to find her. Can you get the police station on the phone for me, please."

Lea pressed a stored number on the switchboard phone and handed it to Ryan.

"Bindarra Creek Police Station. Senior Constable Taylor speaking."

"Abby. It's Ryan. I think we have a problem."

##

Two hours had passed and Jaclyn hadn't turned up. Abby Taylor had stopped Ryan heading off on a wild goose chase by himself.

"We have no idea where they went. For all you know he could have taken her back to Sydney. I can't afford to have you get lost too, and then we'll have a double search on our hands. I know it's hard, Ryan, but be patient. The SES are setting up a search headquarters on the school oval, and I've got reinforcements coming over from Tamworth." Abby squeezed his arm.

"Thanks, Abby." Ryan looked at his watch. It was nine thirty already but a crowd was gathering around the command tent.

"Look, I know very well how hard the waiting is, but it will make for a much more efficient search. We've already done a search of the RMS database and we know what sort of vehicle and its number plate and that information has already been broadcast from here to Sydney. Every police vehicle on the road will be watching out for it, and it's been put on the area command Facebook page too. They'll be spotted soon, don't worry." Abby left him and walked over to Kel Jones.

Ryan looked around. Half the town seemed to have appeared. Dave, the deputy from the high school was flanked by four of the male teachers and Mandy Kaminsky. As the group walked towards the tent, Ryan recognised many other faces, and a surge of gratitude settled in his chest. Rob from the post office and his son, Dan, stood shoulder to shoulder, Jon Kendall stood next to the Sullivan brothers and Jake Morgan.

As he looked around at the crowd, a guy he

didn't recognise came up beside him and held out his hand.

"Ryan, we haven't met yet. I'm Roman Taylor, Abby's husband."

Ryan took his hand and shook it. "Thanks for helping out, Roman. Appreciate it."

Kel Jones picked up the microphone that was attached to a portable PA system. "Gather round, please. I'd like to thank you all for coming out at such short notice. I knew I could depend on our community when we heard that Jaclyn was missing. We're about to get underway." Ryan turned away as Kel outlined the search area; he was going in the police paddy wagon with Abby and AJ.

He walked through the gathered crowd towards the car park where the paddy wagon was parked. Different scenarios flickered though his mind like a horror movie. They'd been gone for twenty-four hours; they could have gotten as far as Queensland or Victoria in that time.

If Jaclyn had been able to, she would have called him. Ryan kicked himself for not coming into town last night; they could have been searching for hours by now.

He pressed the speed dial to Jaclyn's number again, but as it had since last night, it went straight to voicemail. Ryan swallowed and put his hand over his eyes. If that mongrel had hurt her—

"What's wrong, mister. You okay? What's going on here?"

A young boy in a hoodie with a thin face and dark eyes stood in front of him. He reeked of cigarette smoke.

Ryan looked at him; it was that young delinquent from the school who'd caused the problems last week. "The SES is setting up a search headquarters."

"Cool, can I help?" He patted his pocket. "You look like shit. Wanna smoke?"

"No, thanks, I don't smoke. Appreciate the offer, mate, but you've probably got a class to go to."

"Nah, I was gonna skip maths. Hate old Curly, he picks on me. What are they looking for?"

"Ms Douglas is missing."

"Ms Douglas, the new principal?'The boy's eyes widened. "I know where she is. Or where she was yesterday. I wondered what she was doing out there. I wondered why she was going out to Mt Yarrie instead of school. I was hopin' that they hadn't been out to see my old man. I'm in enough trouble at home without the school sticking their bit in again." He shrugged. "But who gives a shit? I don't."

"Out where." Ryan leaned forward. "You saw her? Are you sure? When?"

"Yeah, we was waiting for the bus to school yesterday and I was having a smoke and she frowned at me as they went past, I mean friggin' hell, why can't a man have a smoke in his own time? No school rules on my road."

Ryan stared at him. "This is really important, mate. Are you telling the truth?"

"Yea, bloody oath I am."

"Where was it and what time?"

"Out on Johnsons Loop Road. I live way out in the scrub under Mt Yarrie. It would have been after eight because the bus hadn't come."

"Thank you. That's really helpful."

"Is there a reward?"

"If we find her out there, I'll make sure I look out for you, mate." He squeezed the boy's shoulder and turned away to hurry back to Abby and Kel.

"Wait up," the boy called. "There's more, mister. The car she was in passed the school bus when we were nearly to Bindarra Creek, but the guy was by himself.

"What sort of car was it? Are you sure it was the same one?"

"Yup. A white station wagon. It had black and white number plates. 'PH'. We just did that in science the other day so I remembered it."

##

Within ten minutes a convoy of cars set out for Johnson's Loop Road and Mt Yarrie. Ryan had run towards his ute, but Abby had sent AJ after him.

"Abby said she wants you to come with us in the wagon, man."

A cold feeling settled in Ryan's chest. He knew what was behind it; Abby didn't want him out there alone if there was something bad to be found.

He blocked those thoughts from his mind and followed AJ back to the police wagon.

"This is the quickest way to Mt Yarrie," Abby said as they turned on to the main Tamworth road. They travelled on that road for a few kilometres and the silence was tense. Ryan pulled out his phone and tried Jaclyn's number again. He leaned forward as it rang for the first time, his heart pounding and his mouth dry. He waited for her to answer, when it didn't go straight to voice mail, but there was a crackle and it dropped out again.

"Bloody hell," he muttered.

Abby glanced over her shoulder to the back seat where he was sitting. "What's wrong?"

"I called Jac's number again and it didn't go to voicemail this time, but it dropped out again."

"Okay, now that there's signal, we'll try and locate her phone. I hope she's got location services turned on."

Abby picked up the mike, but before she could

speak the police channel on the two-way radio crackled.

"Bindarra Creek base station. Calling Senior Constable Taylor. Abby, pick up please."

Ryan recognised Riley Morgan, the senior sergeant's voice.

"Go ahead, Riley," Abby said.

Ryan craned forward.

"We've located the car and Peter Hughes. He was picked up at Scone and the detectives are interviewing him now."

"No sign of Jaclyn?"

"No, and they said he denies even seeing her."

"He's got a short memory. He spoke to Lea, and he won't know that Terry Parch saw them together. You make sure they don't let him go."

"No fear of that, Abby."

Abby turned the wagon on to a rutted dirt road. Ryan jumped as his phone vibrated once in his hand and he looked down at the screen. "Abby! My phone just buzzed. It was Jac's number but it's dropped out again." He looked at his service bars. "Hell, we've gone out of service."

Abby picked up the mike and radioed the station. "Riley, we're out of phone service here but Ryan just had a call from Jaclyn's phone before it dropped out. Can you keep trying to call her number please?"

"Will do. We'll stay in touch."

"Okay, guys. That's the bus stop where Terry saw the car go past. Keep your eyes peeled in the bush. We'll go to the top and then come back down. It's only six kilometres until the road ends at the peak."

Ryan stared through the window as Abby slowed the car.

"We're going to the top and Kel's going to get the search teams into the bush from the bus stop to the peak. If she's here, we'll find her."

Chapter 22

Jaclyn turned her phone off and pushed it into her bag.

So close.

She leaned back against the rock wall at the side of the dirt road and looked at her swollen foot. No matter how much it hurt, she had to get to the top of the peak. And when she got there, that's where she'd stay.

Until Ryan came for her.

When her phone had rung for the first time and she had seen Ryan's number, the relief had been sweet. She was trying to preserve her phone battery until she could get to the top of the peak. It was about five hundred metres above, and she prayed there would be consistent service up there. There was no point leaving her phone on; it would deplete the battery charge more quickly as it tried to connect to a network.

She had no doubt that he would. She had no chance of walking down the hill, and the thirty whatever kilometres it was to Tamworth; she just had to preserve her water until help arrived.

The problem was that she hadn't seen a vehicle

or a person since she'd hidden from Peter in the bush yesterday. As she'd heard him coming and caught a glimpse of his white car, she'd run off the side of the road. Her ankle had twisted on the edge of the bank and she'd tumbled down the steep incline, and ended up half in the creek.

Her ankle throbbed now as she pushed herself to her feet and leaned on the stick that she'd used since yesterday to help her limp along. Her progress had been painstakingly slow. It had taken a couple of hours to pull herself up to the road from the creek. Peter's car hadn't slowed, but she'd waited for a half hour before she'd filled her water bottle hoping that the water was as clean as it looked. The creek bubbled from a spring in the side of the hill, and she'd drunk several handfuls from her scooped hands yesterday and hadn't been sick so far.

The trek up the road towards the peak had been painful, and it had started to get dark before she was anywhere near the top. She'd looked around for a sheltered spot within sight of the road, and took off her damp—from her fall into the creek—jacket and leaned against the rock that divided the small clearing from the road. Sleep had been fitful but she'd been encouraged by the lights of a town in the distance and she'd known she was looking out over Bindarra Creek.

Her new home. And the place where Ryan was.

As the sun had cleared the horizon, she'd sat back and looked at the dawn colours of the bush as they changed from dusky pink to amber to the dry brown of drought-stricken paddocks. It was strange considering her dilemma, but serenity filled her as she looked over the countryside that she now called home. She wondered which of the distant farmhouses was Ryan's, and she knew she had to have faith that she would see it one day soon.

Jaclyn had eaten the last half of her muesli bar, and had a quarter of the bottle of creek water before she made her way slowly up the hill, putting her weight on her right foot and the stick. Progress was slow but hope flared in her as she reached the bend and looked down at the road below. Several puffs of dust indicated that more than one vehicle was heading her way.

Walking as quickly as she could to get away from the narrow neck of the road where it curved close to the sheer drop on the left, she gritted her teeth and ignored the pain in her ankle as she reached a flat section close to the peak.

Fighting back tears, she lowered herself to the dirt and took out her phone. Turning it on, she smiled as four bars of signal lit up.

She tried Ryan's number first, but it went to voicemail. Her second call was to the school, and the tears that she'd held back spilled from her eyes when Kellie answered the phone.

"Bindara Cr—"

"Kellie, it's me, Jaclyn. I need help."

Kellie's shriek reverberated through the phone. "Oh my God, Lea, come quick. It's Jaclyn. Oh Jesus, Jaclyn we thought you were bloody dead."

Jaclyn couldn't help the smile that came through the tears. "I'm far from that, Kellie."

"Jaclyn, it's Lea, tell me where you are. There are search parties out looking for you all over. Are you all right?"

"I'm at the top of Mt Yarrie. Well, almost to the top but I've hurt my ankle."

"Just a minute, stay on the phone." Lea's voice was muffled, but Jaclyn could hear her telling Kellie to call Sergeant Morgan immediately. "I'm back now, Jaclyn. I'll stay on the phone with you until someone gets there. Now tell me, are you hurt anywhere else?"

"Just my pride is hurt, and my faith in people is a bit dented." Jaclyn sat up straight; if she leaned forward she could see the dust from one vehicle getting closer.

"You're sure? Are you dehydrated? I'm sure Riley will call the paramedics too."

"No, tell him not to. I'm fine and I can wait until I get back to town." Jaclyn held the phone to her ear with her shoulder and opened her water bottle. She drained the rest of the water. "How did they know where to look for me? I can see the SES hi-vis shirts at the bottom of the hill."

"Terry Parch saw you go past yesterday. God love him, it's probably the only decent thing he's done in his life, but he's getting some street cred out of it."

"I owe him. It's very lonely up here. I haven't seen another person in twenty-four hours."

"It won't be long now. Kellie's got onto the sergeant and he's radioed Abby. They'll be with you soon."

"I can hear a vehicle coming now. Thanks Lea. I'll see you soon."

"Take care, love. We've missed you. Even Deputy Dave's been out searching for you. You've made a big impact on the school and the community in a very short time." Lea's voice shook, and that brought fresh tears to Jaclyn's eyes as she put the phone back in her bag. Taking a deep breath, she wiped her eyes and then pushed herself to her feet with her trusty stick as the police paddy wagon came around the bend. It pulled up in a cloud of dust and Jaclyn blinked as the car door slammed and Ryan rushed towards her.

"Jac!"

His arms went around her and she rested her head on his shoulder for a few seconds before he stepped back.

"Are you hurt, sweetheart?" His fingers were gentle on her arms as he held her eyes with his.

"I'm fine. Just a sore ankle, but it's not too bad. I managed to walk up the mountain with it. I knew I'd get a signal up here."

"I've been trying to call all morning, but it dropped out the one time we almost connected. When you got through to Lea they'd just pinpointed your location using your phone." Ryan rested his forehead against hers as Abby and AJ waited near the police vehicle. "I thought I'd lost you again, Jac. I'm not going to wait any longer. I want us to be together all of the time. You know how you said you were going to buy your own place in town? I want to ask if you could cope with living in a ramshackle old farmhouse? It's nothing like your apartment, but—"

Jaclyn lifted her head and pressed her lips against those of the man she loved. "We can talk about it later. Abby and AJ are waiting for us."

"Hang onto your handbag."

She smiled as Ryan scooped his hands beneath her legs and lifted her into his arms.

Epilogue

18 months later

The hall was packed and the crowd was buzzing with excitement. The red curtains on the stage were closed but occasionally a child's head would peer through the gap in the centre. Jaclyn leaned over and whispered in Ryan's ear. "Look, even the Parches are here." She nodded to the row in front of them.

"The whole town is here," he replied, squeezing her hand.

Jaclyn sat back and ran her hand over her tight stomach.

"You okay, love?" Ryan frowned as Jaclyn tried to get comfortable on the plastic school chair.

"All good. The baby's not due for three weeks, so he's getting settled. Oooh!" She jumped and grinned as a heel pushed underneath her ribs.

Ryan smiled back at her and Jaclyn's heart swelled with love for her husband of one year. "Or *she's* getting settled."

"Nope, definitely a soccer player."

"Girls play soccer too. You're sure you're okay?" Ryan reached over and touched her stomach. "We can go home or straight to the hospital if you need to?"

"No way. I'm not missing this for the world. And I'm fine! This is normal."

"Okay. You should be up on the stage with Dave."

"No. I'm on maternity leave and he's doing a great job." As the curtains opened and the hall lights dimmed, Jaclyn looked up at the stage where once "Derro" Dave was sitting beside the regional director. She and Dave had come to have a great working relationship in the eight months they'd worked together before Jaclyn had taken maternity leave. So good, she'd had no hesitation taking leave when she got too uncomfortable to drive to school each day.

Life had settled into a happy routine after her kidnap. Peter Hughes was in jail—charged with kidnapping—but the fifty thousand dollars he had stolen from her previous school had not been found, and he'd denied any wrongdoing, despite telling Jaclyn he had been responsible.

Jaclyn had set aside her angst, even though Peter's words had been true. She had never received an apology from the department even after he had been jailed. In the way life—and love—had panned out, it wasn't important. The situation had brought her to Bindarra Creek and reunited her with Ryan. That alone had made it all worthwhile.

Living out on Ryan's farm had been a huge change for Jaclyn, but she loved every minute of it. The renovations at the farm had occurred faster than the restoration at the school. They were here to attend the opening ceremony tonight.

"Yes, ssh. Jaclyn, pay attention." The wavering voice of her grandmother came from her left, and Jaclyn nodded.

"Yes, Gran." One of the best things about settling in Bindarra Creek was that as soon as Gran had found out Jaclyn was moving to the country, she'd asked if they could find her a place in the aged care facility in Bindarra. "It makes sense, it saves you coming all that way to visit, and I can be here when you produce my new great granddaughter."

"Or great grandson," Jaclyn had said. "Why is everyone so sure I'm having a girl!"

"Because you are," Gran had said.

Jaclyn was happy and content and being able to hand over to Dave without worry had been a joy.

Someone tapped her shoulder and she half-turned around. Abby and Roman were sitting behind them.

"Are you okay, Jac? You're doing an awful lot of squirming in your seat.

"I'm fine," Jaclyn whispered as the school band started playing. "Um, I think." Abby and Roman

247

had become close friends over the past year.

Once the band had finished and the audience—including Jaclyn— had risen for the national anthem, the regional director stood and crossed to the lectern.

"It gives me great pleasure to be here tonight to celebrate the official opening of the new specialist block—or should I say refurbished block—at Bindarra Creek Central School. After some more items by the students, we'll tour the new facility, and I'll ask your principal—even though she is on leave—to cut the ribbon and then we'll all come back here for a supper provided by the CWA ladies."

Jaclyn sat up straight as the hard back of the chair pressed into her and caused a cramp in her side. Both Gran and Ryan shot her a look and Jaclyn stared ahead paying attention to the director.

"But first I'd like to say a few words," he continued. "I am sure that this community is well aware of the fine principal you have. Jaclyn Rossiter—then Ms Douglas—came to this community under difficult circumstances almost two years ago, and she has done her utmost to make Bindarra Creek the best school she could." He looked down to the third row where Jaclyn was seated. "Mrs Rossiter, I'd like to ask you to come up and join us on the stage. I have something to give you."

Jaclyn frowned, but Ryan stood and helped her up before leading her to the stage. She waddled up the two steps and smiled at the director as he handed her an envelope.

"Over the past six months," he said. "We have examined data and results from our rural schools statewide. I'm pleased to announce under your leadership, Mrs Rossiter"—he turned and nodded to Dave—"and Mr Kepple, that Bindarra Creek has been chosen as one of the top five rural schools of excellence in New South Wales. It gives me great pleasure to present the certificate to Mrs Rossiter. Without you, this wouldn't have happened."

The audience broke into applause, and Terry Parch whistled from his seat in the front row. "Go, Jac!" he yelled, and Jaclyn smothered a smile.

"Would you like to say a few words to your school community, Jaclyn?"

"I would. I have two very brief things to say tonight. First, I'm extremely proud of this school, and I love being a part of the Bindarra Creek community. The growth in the school has been due to the tremendous community support we receive." She paused and drew in a deep breath as her stomach tightened again. "The staff is dedicated, and the students work hard. All of those things contribute to our fine results. I'm here to stay."

There was more loud applause and another piercing whistle from Terry Parch who had been Jaclyn's shadow since he had contributed to her rescue. It was a slow process but he was gradually becoming a better student.

She held the microphone out to the director and drew in a deep breath as another sharp cramp gripped her.

"And the second?" he asked quietly.

Jaclyn lifted the microphone and looked down at the two people she loved.

"Um, the second thing?" She clutched her stomach. "Ryan, will you take me to the hospital, please?"

Ryan was up on the stage before she had handed the microphone back to a stunned director.

##

Ava Beth Rossiter was delivered safely at the Bindarra Creek hospital just over an hour later. The community members had toured and admired the new buildings and were still enjoying Gemma Haydon's scones when Ava was placed in her mother's arms.

Jaclyn held Ryan's gaze as she held their daughter for the first time. 'You were all right. We have a little girl."

"A beautiful daughter, just like her mother."

Ryan leaned over and brushed his lips over Jaclyn's forehead. "I love you, Jac. I'm very happy you followed me to Bindarra Creek."

Jaclyn smiled as Ryan shifted his gaze to their newborn daughter. "It was worth the wait," he whispered.

THE END

Bindarra Creek A Town Reborn

Welcome to Bindarra Creek, a struggling country town where people work hard and love deeply. Set in the picturesque tablelands of New England, Australia, Bindarra Creek is a fictional, drought stricken community full of intrigue, adventure, drama and romance.

Life and love in a small country town has never been more challenging.

Bindarra Creek A Town Reborn series consists of eight romances written by nine Australian authors and published individually (beginning in July 2019).

In order of release:

Take Me Home – Suzanne Gilchrist (aka S E Gilchrist)
In the Heat of the Night – Susanne Bellamy
No Looking Back - Linda Charles
Worth the Wait – Annie Seaton
With Every Breath – Lauren K. McKellar
Stealing Her Heart – Simone Angela
A Twist of Fate – Erin Moira O'Hara
Promise Me Forever – Juanita Kees

~

To date there are three group writing venture 'series' set in our fictional small town of Bindarra Creek all written by best-selling Australian romance authors. Our latest series is A **Town Reborn.** An anthology of short romances, **Bindarra Creek Short & Sweet,** was released in January 2019 and our first series, **A Bindarra Creek Romance,** was released during

2015/2016.

All books are available as ebooks, some also have paperback versions.

Each series has one theme running throughout, while every romance depicts the changing lives of the townsfolk as our small town begins to grow and thrive despite the dramas of everyday life.

Bindarra Creek Short & Sweet Anthology comprised of:

What's in a Kiss – Linda Charles
My Forever Valentine – Sandie James
Pearls and Green Beer – Susanne Bellamy
Full Circle – Annie Seaton
Date with Destiny – Erin Moira O'Hara
A Letter From the Queen – Lee Christine
Love's Sweet Challenge – Suzanne Gilchrist (aka S E Gilchrist)
The Widow Maker – Lauren K. McKellar
Out of the Blue – Noelle Clark

~

Books in the first **Bindarra Creek Romance series:**

Bindarra Creek Makeover - S. E. Gilchrist

Shadows of the Heart　 - Lee Christine

Second Chance Love - Susanne Bellamy

The CEO Mechanic - Sandie James

Reach for the Stars - Kerrie Paterson

Home to Bindarra Creek - Juanita Kees

Stolen Sanctuary - Stacey Nash

Tempting Fate - Erin Moira O'Hara

One More Day - Linda Charles

The Vine - Lauren K. McKellar

The Ghost of His Past - Simone Angela

Joanie's Dilemma - Marianne Theresa

Buckley's Chance - Noelle Clark

For more info on Bindarra Creek Romances, please visit

www.bindarracreekromance.com

~

Acknowledgements

As always, thank you to my editor, Susanne Bellamy and proof reader, Roby Aiken.

*

About the Author

Author of the Year Ausrom Readers' Choice 2014

Best Established Author Ausrom Readers' Choice 2015

Finalist for Author of the Year, Book of the Year, Cover of the Year, Ausrom Readers' Choice 2016

Best Established Author, Ausrom Readers' Choice 2017

Book of the Year. Ausrom Readers' Choice 2018

Annie lives in Australia, on the beautiful north coast of New South Wales. She sits in her writing chair and looks out over the tranquil Pacific Ocean. She has fulfilled her lifelong dream of becoming an author and is producing books at a prolific rate.

She writes contemporary romance and loves telling the stories that always have a happily ever after. She lives with her very own hero of many years and they share their home with Toby, the naughtiest dog in the universe, and Barney, the rag doll kitten, who hides when the grandchildren come to visit.

Stay up to date with her latest releases at her website: http://www.annieseaton.net

If you would like to stay up to date with Annie's releases, subscribe to her newsletter on her website.

Other Books by Annie Seaton

Porter Sisters Series
Kakadu Sunset
Daintree
Diamond Sky
Hidden Valley (2021)

Pentecost Island Series (2020)
Pippa
Eliza
Nell
Tamsin
Evie

Cherry
Odessa
Sienna
Tess
Isla

Bondi Beach Love Series

Beach House
Beach Music
Beach Walk
Beach Dreams

The House on the Hill Boxed Set

Prickle Creek Series
Her Outback Cowboy
Her Outback Surprise
His Outback Nanny
His Outback Temptation

Second Chance Bay Series
Her Outback Playboy
Her Outback Protector
Her Outback Haven
Her Outback Paradise

Love Across Time Series
Come Back to Me
Follow Me
Finding Home

The Threads that Bind (2021)

Others

Whitsunday Dawn
Undara
The Trouble with Paradise
The Trouble with Jack

Deadly Secrets
Adventures in Time
Silver Valley Witch
The Emerald Necklace
Ten Days in Tuscany
Worth the Wait
Full Circle

*

WORTH THE WAIT
Copyright © 2019 ANNIE SEATON

Cover Design by: Paradox Designs

Editors: Susanne Bellamy, R.L.Aiken

.